Nuclear Autumn

A Tale from the Mike Side

Michael Kent

ISBN: 10: 0-9989990-4-0
ISBN-13: 978-0-9989990-4-3

OTHER BOOKS BY MICHAEL KENT

The Haunting of Molly Pickett
Three Days after the Cross
Growing through the Cracks of Adversity
The Family Business
Deranged

Available on Amazon & Kindle
Audiobooks available at TalesFromTheMikeSide.com

CHAPTER 1

Jan 1908
Sheffield England

Burling Payne paced around the ostentatious desk in his big game trophy room. Burling was a large bear of a man. His young wife, Jane, was known in social circles as a commoner because she did her own cooking; which is why Burling married her. Jane had been his field cook on several safaris.

"Left turns only, Burling?"

"Left turns, for luck," he answered as he circled the desk wearing a smoking jacket he'd long outgrown.

"Well, it worked. Your package is here. But the courier won't let me sign for it. So come along. I don't suppose you'll be taking me shopping in London this week?"

"I've spoiled you, Jane. Maybe next week."

A uniformed courier stood shivering, on the concrete porch, with a cardboard tube under his arm.

"Package from Professor Falkner. Are you Burling…"

Burling didn't mean to be rude.

"Yes, yes!"

"Sign here please."

Burling kissed the package as he returned to his trophy room, where he cleared the center of the big mahogany desk, and slowly opened it.

"Look at it, Jane. Isn't it magnificent?"

"A fine sight indeed. No pun intended."

They both laughed as he unscrewed the cover caps from the telescopic sights.

Burling selected his fine Remington rolling block rifle from its cradle and examined it for several minutes. He then spent the remainder of the afternoon attaching the sight to the thirty-inch, tapered octagon cobalt-blue barrel.

"I'll be out for a walk, Jane. I may be awhile."

"Couldn't even wait until morning, could you?"

"You know me all too well. Here's a kiss." he said and pecked his wife on the cheek.

Jane wiped sweat from a day in the kitchen from her drooping red locks.

"Too long and your mutton will be tough."

CHAPTER 2

Feb 1908
Cambridge England

Professor Cedric Falkner rubbed tension from the back of his fifty-five-year old neck. A younger astronomer looked over Cedric's shoulder as he peered into the aperture of the Northumberland telescope at the Cambridge University Observatory.

"May I have a look, Cedric?" Armando Calossi asked, with an Italian accent. "It's almost out of sight."

"Oh, Sorry"

Falkner stood and let Armando take the observer's chair.

"My neck is sore anyway."

Armando brushed aside his long black hair and studied the visage.

"You say he found this through a rifle sight?"

"Not just any rifle sight," Falkner boasted. "I ground the lenses myself. He could see a humming bird at a thousand yards."

"And you say he claimed to see it split?"

"I've known Burling Payne for thirty-five years. Not only do I trust his word, but his account made perfect since. Fuzzy object... just above Venus...grew brighter...separated into two fuzzy objects; one bright, one dim."

Armando turned to his mentor.

"What are the odds of a riflemen aiming at an undiscovered comet, during the very moment that it split in two?"

The older man gave a twirl to an end of his gray handlebar mustache for effect.

"Well let's just give it a go. He received the well-wrapped package containing the telescope late that afternoon. Knowing Burling, he opened it with extreme caution. Say it took an hour to inspect and mount the scope. He would have hiked a mile into Hollow Meadows, straight away, to calibrate his shooting distance. He'd take aim at the treetops in Royde's Clough, to the east just after sunset…"

Armando stood and put a hand on Cedric's shoulder.

"No need to mock me, Professor. With Venus at zenith, it would be almost impossible for him not to see it."

CHAPTER 3

Mar 1908
Cambridge England

Four of Cambridge University's finest astronomic scholars sat with administrators, in the provost's antechamber, jockeying for preeminence. Master Edington played the peacemaker.

"Be reasonable, Professor Falkner. This institution has gone out on a limb for you before."

"Water on Mars!" Sir Gregory grumbled.

"And life on Mars!" Dame Carol added, with laughter.

Edington seemed cautious, but pliable.

"No one else has seen it, Cedric. What are we to do?"

"Armando saw it! He swore to it!"

The Dame was still laughing.

"He swore there was life on Mars! No other observatory has reported seeing it."

Falkner pounded a fist on the big table.

"And they won't see it! 2140 is eclipsing Venus, with its tail pointing toward the sun."

Gregory looked down through spectacles that sat on the edge of his nose.

"And why was it not observed prior to the eclipse?"

"Because no one was looking; not even us!"

"Oh that's right," Carol smirked. "Your rifleman friend spotted it with his spyglass."

Provost Gallanter was a sickly man who disdained heated arguments.

"Let's all calm down. Let Professor Falkner make his case."

Falkner leaned forward, with his elbows on the table.

"No one will see it. Not until it's too late. Venus is almost in superior conjunction."

Dame Carol looked at Sir Gregory, who whispered,

"Passing behind the sun."

"2140 will be in the sun's glare for months. We must warn the world."

The Provost forbade it.

"Under no circumstances will this university announce that an unseen comet will strike the earth. Not until we're sure. And how can anyone be so sure? It would be like a bullet striking a bullet."

"Bullets do not have predictable orbits," Cedrick clarified. "And neither do they have gravity. I have plotted 2140's ten-thousand-year orbit."

Sir Gregory stood up.

"I've heard enough. Ten-thousand years, with earth-sized precision is impossible."

Falkner rose, towering over the shorter man.

"And you sir, are cautious to the point of idiocy. The Mayans did it without modern telescopes. The world must, and I say *must*, be told."

Dame Carol shook her head.

"Now I've heard it all."

Her sentiment resonated with her peers. Provost Gallanter remained seated.

"Cedric, we've been friends for sixteen years. I'm warning you. Don't do this."

CHAPTER 4

Heavenly eyes looked on as an icy chunk of cosmic flotsam approached the orbits of the inner planets. A legion of angels convened in earth's stratosphere. The Archangel, Gabriel, posed a question.

"Is there anyone among us who does not know what that is?"

The Guardian Angel, Pavilax, was numbered with those that did not. And Gabriel said thusly:

"In the beginning, God created the heavens and the earth. The earth was a dark water planet, heated by a super molten core. And the Spirit of God hovered, expectantly, upon the face of the liquid deep. And because God looked lovingly upon the earth, a rebellious angel sought to destroy it.

Satan watched as God set the parameters for earth's solar system, knowing that the earth was orbiting a solar mass that would eventually ignite under the crush of God's most immutable physical force; gravity. At the far outer reaches of the fledgling system lie a spherical cloud of planetoid sized objects. If pushed ever so slightly from such a distance, a small planetoid could be nudged precisely into a decaying solar orbit that would strike God's favored place, in the distant future.

God, knowing all things, allowed his created servants, led by Satan, to do as they willed. His omnipotent plan would prevail, and they would be punished, according to the magnitude of their sin.

In the interim between demonic cause and earthly effect, God created microscopic organisms to ingest water molecules, and isolate the atomic Oxygen. The Oxygen atoms powered these microbes and they percolated from the vast magma heated ocean, giving off Carbon Dioxide as waste once they reached the surface. Thusly, a rudimentary gaseous carbon dioxide atmosphere formed over the warm ocean.

Satan roiled a portion of God's first life forms, causing them to turn on their precursors, thereby creating earth's first parasites. Spawned in darkness they were designed to feed on God's microbes. As they rose to the surface the parasites stole their atomic Oxygen; killing them and stifling the production of an atmosphere.

And thus it was so for eons, until God said "Let there be Light." The sun lurched with the birthing pangs of nuclear fusion, as Satan's comet entered the inner solar system. God, in His Trinity, laughed as the comet skimmed the thin carbon dioxide atmosphere and slingshot back toward deep space.

The dark star of a sun crushed atomic hydrogen into helium, erupting into a single fusion flare. The sun caught fire as if lit by a torch. Eight minutes later, ninety-three million miles away, a mega-burst of pristine sunlight penetrated the depths of the ocean, killing every single demon spawned parasite on earth. And God said the light was good.

CHAPTER 5

30 Jun 1908
Easter Siberian

The brothers, Chekan and Chuchan, stooped in a blind, just downstream, from their log hunting hut. These hunters from the Shanyagir tribe were dressed in buckskins. Their clothes and faces were smeared with charcoal for camouflage amongst narrow spruce tree trunks along the banks of the Podkamennaya Tunguska River. The morning air was brisk for this time of year.

The younger brother, Chekan, loaded a single bottlenecked cartridge into the breach of his Mosin–Nagant hunting rifle.
"Shhhh," his older brother whispered.
Chekan closed the bolt and took aim at a sixteen-point bull elk, less than fifty meters away, on the other side of the river.
KA-RACK.

Chuchan gave Chekan a heavy handed slap on the back.
"Good shot."
Chekan's back stung as much as his shooting shoulder.
"Now go skin it, you oaf."
"Follow me," Chuchan laughed, and bolted toward the footbridge.

Their baby sister, Kamen, came running around the bend to meet them.
"Can we go home now?" She shouted, while holding up her tattered dress.

They converged, all panting at the footbridge, where Chuchan laughingly told their sister:

"Yes, if your husband still wants you."

"Always the oaf," Chekan said, defending their sister. "Leave her alone."

"Is it the big buck?" She asked, looking at Chekan.

"Yes," Chekan answered. "Help us dress him before he gets cold."

*****

Elk flesh lie exposed along the animal's flank. Chekan pulled back the pelt while Chuchan skinned toward the backbone. Kamen knelt skinning the elk's front leg, as buzzards circled high overhead. She wiped sweat and elk musk from her brow.

"Those buzzards are going to eat your ugly face, Chuchan."

Her senses were jarred when thousands of birds launched from their perches and took flight. In a moment, the sky was darkened by clouds of flocks, all flying in the same direction. She dropped her skinning blade and stood staring at the sky.

"Where are they going?"

A bluish green fireball carved the sky in two, like some heavenly dagger that grew brighter than the sun. Kamen shielded her eyes, thinking that the world was ending. The air was growing unbearably hot. She felt the heat spike as the fireball roared overhead with the sound of falling rocks.

The first explosion knocked the siblings off their feet. Three more explosions in quick succession set the ground a-sway. A hot wind swept by, snapping off the treetops. Kamen thought the sky was falling. She screamed, but she couldn't hear herself. In her confusion, and seeking to find shelter, she made a wobbling dash for the cabin. She felt hands grab each of her arms as her brothers came alongside her and dragged her, sloshing, into the shallows and under the wooden bridge.

"Duck under!" Chekan yelled.

The water was warm, but cooler than the air above it. Kamen took a deep breath and slipped under the water. Eyes open, she held her breath. In a moment a booming underwater shockwave crushed the air from her lungs and sent her flailing upriver, awash with the planks of the pulverized bridge. Black shards from the fallen sky, pierced the water all around her.

Kamen struggled to right herself after tumbling under water for almost too long. She stuck her head above water that was almost too hot, and heaved in a long breath.

"Chekan! Chuchan!"

The river stopped and washed back in the other direction. Kamen, beaten bloody by wooden planks, pulled herself onto the riverbank, lest she be killed in the backwash.

CHAPTER 6

Tomsk Station, Siberia
30 Jun 1928

The Trans-Siberian Express was thirty-eight hours out of Moscow when it chugged into the Tomsk station. Just days past the summer solstice the sun was just setting at 10:00 pm. A beleaguered party of seven climbed down from coach car sixteen and tramped through the mud, toward the station, beside the red wheeled engine with four funnels. Heat from the boilers warmed Professor Cedrick Falkner's seventy-five-year old bones from the evening drizzle as they approached.

"I'd rather walk in the mud than wade through all those passengers," Cedrick professed, tightening the collar on a coat made for British winters. "I'll be fine."

"Here old man, let me help you along," his old friend, Burling Payne offered.

"Get your hands off me. You're almost as old as I am."

Burling's wife, Jane, was sixteen years his junior, at fifty-four.

"Well I'm not. Here let me help you."

"Much preferred, to that old coot of a husband of yours."

Three younger men, one little more than a lad, followed with some of their bags. Three Kazaks in robes and turbans stood at the beginning of the train station's boardwalk.

"Unsavory looking characters," Cedrick mumbled.

Burling coughed at him.

"Mind your mouth, Sir Cedrick. You're not in Cambridge anymore."

Their young translator said something in a language Cedrick didn't

16

understand, and the Mongolians stepped aside. Cedrick thanked him.

"Good show then, Leonardo."

"It's why you hired me, isn't it?"

The engine seemed to relax as it sought thermodynamic equilibrium. Thick black smoke still bellowed from the funnels, and white steam through the boiler relief valves. The train station was an unimpressive, single story, half log and half brick building. Probably amid modernization. The tavern, in a separate building, beyond the ticket booth and the trading post was conspicuous. And the two elder men made straight for it.

"One drink. That and no more!" Jane called out as they rushed away.

The tavern was lively, with accordion music and wanton women. The local men, made obvious from the smut of hard labor, eyed the transient passengers like vultures.

"Janes right, Cedrick." Burling warned. "One drink."

"Hold onto your wallet." Cedrick mumbled as they bellied up to the bar. "Schnapps. One for me; one for my friend."

The bar tender slammed a bottle in front of them.

"Wodka!" He roared, to the laughter of locals.

"Well then," Cedrick capitulated. "Two vodkas."

The indigenous stared while the bar tender poured. *Must be a joke*, Cedrick thought. But his eyes widened in pain when the drink hit his throat. And the locals laughed, pounding on the bar.

Burling's throat fared better, or at least he pretended it to.

"Come on then. We don't want your wife to come looking for us."

"Hold on." Came the voice of a stranger.

A large rugged looking man squeezed in beside Cedrick as he turned to leave. He spoke English, with a heavy Russian accent.

"Have one more, on me."

"Sorry; no time."

The Russian flipped his pocket watch on its chain, caught it, and opened it.

"Twenty-eight more minutes till train leaves. Plenty of time. Tri Wodki."

"Tri Wodki, Vladimere." The bar tender repeated, before filling their shot glasses, and pouring one for the stranger.

"I am Vladimir."

Burling hoisted his glass, and yelled over the raucous crowd of men and bar girls.

"I'm Burling. This is Sir Cedrick. A toast – to Vladimir."

Cedrick tried not to flinch this time. But the Russian's slap on the back startled him, and he regurgitated in his glass. The Russian laughed.

"What brings you men out here to the frontier? Is it the hunt?"

"Burling's the hunter. I'm an astronomer."

"All the way out here, to look through telescope?"

"Do you know what day this is, my good man?"

"Is Saturday," Vladimir answered with a broad grin.

"Not just any Saturday. It's been twenty years, to the day, since the Tunguska event."

"You mean meteor?"

"Not a meteor. A piece of the Comet 2140, from the edge of the solar system."

The Russian's grin was gone.

"Then you two are very brave men."

Sir Cedrick examined the contents of his glass and decided not to drink it.

"Just a merry hike," he said, putting the shot on the bar. "We'll be digging for samples."

"If the tigers don't get you, the Walley People will."

Burling cocked an ear.

"Valley People?"

"Walmpir," the Russian said flatly.

Burling shook his head.

"Vampir? Never heard of them. Are they tribal?"

Vladimir's eyes widened, when he answered,

"Night walkers. Blood suckers. Seducers of soul."

Cedrick heard enough to think the man mad.

"Well then, Mister Vladimir; It's been quite the pleasure. But our train — we have to go."

Vladimir downed the contents of Cedrick's glass and slammed it back on the bar.

"I am serious. If you go, you will not come back. No one does."

Burling intervened on the part of his civil friend.

"And what about you, Vladimir? Why are you out here in this God forsaken place? Hiding, maybe?"

"I am trader."

"A trader of what?"

"Sometimes coffee, from Africa. Sometimes diamonds — *mostly* from Africa. But mainly - protection."

Burling stared him square in the face.

"My Carbine is protection enough."

The Russian almost touched noses with Burling.

"Maybe you get off one shot. Maybe two. But then you will welcome death."

"And you can do better?"

Vladimir nodded slowly.

"I have American machine gun. Shoot one hundred times in ten seconds. Then you maybe have chance."

Burling looked to Cedrick, who answered for both.

"It took me twenty years to save for this expedition. We have two more young men with rifles already."

"They will run. Vladimir will not."

"Then I'm certain we can't afford your services."

"You are right, Sir Cedrick. You cannot afford. But Vladimir will do for free."

Now Cedrick looked to Burling, who asked,

"And why on earth would anyone risk their life for free."

Cedrick had never seen a look like the one on Vladimir's face, when he answered.

"For *sport* of it!"

CHAPTER 7

Irkutsk Station, Siberia
1 July 1928

The Irkutsk station was no more than a log cabin, with a ticket booth and a small trading post. The morning train, from Tomsk, whistled in the distant darkness, some fourteen hours after leaving the station. Jane nudged her husband.

"Do you think he'll show?"

"He didn't seem the sort to go back on his word."

"And the stories? Do you believe the stories?"

"I believe that *he* believes them."

The ground rumbled as the train rounded the foggy bend. The screech of hydraulic brakes pierced the night. One of the young men, a tracker named Brutus, had been bragging all day.

"We've wasted a whole day here, Sir Cedrick. I hope he's worth the wait."

Cedrick waxed sullen.

"Quite the contrary, young man. I hope we won't need him at all."

The train came to a halt with a hissing blast of pressure relief. Their new colleague was last to detrain. His luggage, an army duffle bag and an odd shaped black case, hit the ground ahead of him as he stumbled from the lead coach car.

Cedrick thought it, but Brutus was first to say it:

"He's drunk."

"You're drunk," Cedrick repeated, when Vladimir was in earshot.

"For now," Vladimir answered as he staggered toward the station.
The party grumbled protests, putting Cedrick on the spot.

"It's just unacceptable."

Vladimir gave Cedrick that unfamiliar icy stare, and told him,

"Vladimir will not run. Vladimir will not hide. We sleep here in station?"
Cedrick relented.

"Better inside than out, I suppose."

As comfortable as they could get on benches and the split log floor. Burling whispered to Cedrick.

"That look in his eyes — I've seen it before."

"What does it mean?" Cedrick whispered back.

"He has no conscience. He wouldn't hesitate to kill you."

"You should've said that before we hired him."

"Even worse; we didn't *hire* him. He kills for sport."

*****

The morning mist, over the Angara river, found eight passengers boarding the off-duty ice breaker tug *Perseyet*:
-   Cedrick, the Astronomer.
-   Burling and Jayne Payne.
-   Vladimir, the mercenary.
-   Leonardo, the Italian linguist.
-   The twins, Dornish and Dotz, were Russian bagboys
-   Brutus, the tracker/gunman.

Cedrick bargained with the thick bearded bear of a captain, Ivan Bussie.

"I wired ahead for a bigger boat."

"No bigger boat. Only this boat."

"Seventy-thousand rubles, then?"

"Nyet. Perseyet good boat. One hundred thousand rublis."

Cedrick had no sea legs. He wobbled along, chasing the captain as the Perseyet rocked, not so gently, at the dock.

"Small boat — seventy-thousand rubles."

Captain Bussie weaved nimbly through piles of wound rope, on the narrow deck between the port gunnel and the crew compartment, with clumsy Cedrick close behind. The captain climbed the bridge ladder to the third story wheel house while Cedrick followed him with his eyes. The captain looked up at the single stack of the single engine Koch built ice tug. And then forty-two feet, from aft to stern.

"Is good boat!" He yelled down. "One hundred thousand rublis. No more talk."

Cedrick heard the deep throated diesel engine crank and throttle to idle. As expected, the Russian gunman was last to board. He came stomping down the dock in a long coat, carrying his gear. A gust of wind revealed a holstered, pearl handled revolver. Cedrick studied the man's black case, as Burling asked,

"Is that – a horn case?"

"Is *French* horn case," Vladimir answered with a hearty laugh.

The passengers, all except Vladimir, sat back to back on four steamer trunks as the first mate, Anatoli, pushed off.

"Listen to me!" The captain bellowed. "I say sit – you sit."

Cedrick eyed Vladimir, who slowly took to a deck chair. The captain went on.

"I say stop – you stop. I say go – you go. I tell you get off boat – you get off boat. I tell you get on boat – you get on boat. Understand? I say – you do. No questions. Understand?"

No one answered.

"DO YOU UNDERSTAND!"

Everyone said yes, except for Vladimir, who only nodded. And so they sat, as the Perseyet chugged slowly up-river, with a crew of four.

Jane stared, hypnotized by gentle wake trailing several boat lengths aft. Lulled into a meditative state by the monotonous drone of the engine, she lost all track of time. *Why am I not shopping, in London, for fall fashions. Shopping – that's the ticket.*

Laughter invaded her imaginary shopping spree.

"Burling? What's so funny?

"Turns out, the cabin boy is a girl," her husband laughed.

"Are you all daft? Of course she's a girl."

The skinny, olive skinned young woman in the galley was changing hats. She tossed her men's, fir, ear-hat on a shelf. She re-twisted her long black hair into a bun, to fit under a chef's hat. Jane saw Leonardo smiling. The girl smiled back. But only quaintly. When Jane saw Vladimir leering, she decided the girl could use some company, and joined her in the modest galley.

"What is your name, dear?"

"Madip," the girl answered.

Jane wondered, because of the men's attention to her, and couldn't help but ask:

"How old are you?"

"Twenty-one," the woman answered in a semblance of English.

"You look fifteen," Jane said, and smiled.

"Shanyagir women look much young," Madip replied.

Madip sharpened a fillet knife on a wet-stone, as Jane tried her best to get to know her.

"I'll help you cook," Jane offered. "What will it be?"

"Alexi catch fish. Madip cook fish."

Jane pumped fresh water into the sink and washed her hands.

*****

Meanwhile, there was a commotion on the deck. Brutus was bullying the deck hand into letting him hold an extremely long fishing rod, that had already been cast.

"Come on, give it to me!"

"Nyet!" Alexi protested. "You don't know what you are doing."

"Come on. Let me try."

The captain belly-laughed.

"Give to him!"

And it was so. The long haired twin, Dornish, made sport of the situation.

"We have drama unfolding. Will Brutus catch a fish. Or will we eat salted pork?"

Brutus spat in the water.

"Shut up, bag boy."

Dornish picks fight. I get beat up, Dotz thought.

"Here you go again, Dornish!"

"It's just a joke," Dornish told his brother.

"Will you two be quiet," Brutus snapped. "You'll scare away this fish."

"Don't say anything to him," Dotz whispered.

"Why should I be quiet, when his ugly face is scaring the fish?"

Brutus turned his head.

"Tell you what bagboy…"

"My name is Dornish."

Dotz shook his head. *I'll be bleeding again if he doesn't shut up.*

"He's just joking with you, Brutus."

Brutus wasn't laughing.

"I'll wager both of you Dornish's. If I don't catch a fish I'll give you both five rubles."

"He is Dornish. I am Dotz. I would rather we all get along."
But Dornish had always been the bold one. He wasn't joking anymore.

"And what if you do?"

"I'm gonna beat both of you like drums."
Dornish broke for him. But the Captain and Anatoli snatched him up in mid stride and scolded the three of them.

"Listen, you three…"

"I am not involved," Dotz interrupted.

"…No fighting on boat."
Brutus smiled.

"Oh please let him go."
But the Captain was adamant.

"I tell again – I break your face."

CHAPTER 8

The Perseyet chugged north on the Angara River while Madip and Jane wiped down counter tops and tables. Out of nowhere, Madip blurted:

"Captain will not go on Tunguska River."

"Why not?"

Jane thought it peculiar, when Madip answered.

"Because *I* tell him not go."

Jane only frowned in wonder, as Madip went on.

"Bad place. Valmpir Bad. Valmpir eat Shanyagir people. Valmpir eat many people," she repeated and clicked her teeth together for emphasis.

"Val'pir canibals?"

Madip shook her head.

"Madip not know ca-ni-bal. Shanyagir tribe say it, *Valm-pir.* Valmpir eat Shanyagir."

Madip grabbed Jane by both shoulders.

"Captain not go Tunguska River. You go – you die."

Jane was about to run and tell her husband when the whine of a fishing reel took everyone's attention.

"God in heaven!" Brutus yelled. "Somebody get a net!"

The crew roared with laughter as the long rod bent into a narrow arc – almost pulling Brutus over the side. The men gathered round as Brutus, who was obviously out muscled, struggled to keep his grip on the thick alloy handle.

"You lose rod…" the captain laughed. "You jump in and get."

Brutus went for the quick catch and tired quickly. Muscles bulged under his long-sleeved, flannel pullover, as the would-be catch dragged him along the starboard rail, knocking over onlookers as he went.

"Watch, you oaf," Dornish told him.

Captain Bussie roared with laughter, while several men coached.

"Perhaps you should listen to Alexi," Burling shouted, as Brutus tripped and fell on the steamer trunks.

"Yes, yes," Cedrick agreed. "Let him run."

Anatoli was not as polite.

"Set drag, you idiot!"

Alexi tried to turn a little wheel on the big reel. Jane assumed he was 'setting the drag'. But Brutus pushed him out of the way. For fifteen minutes, Brutus sweat and cursed. And then:

"Is river sturgeon," Alexi shouted, as a spinney dorsal hump appeared and disappeared.

But Brutus was spent. The fishing rod straightened, along with Brutus' arms.

"Give to me," Alexi asked.

He didn't have to ask twice. Brutus, with head held low, relinquished the fish to Alexi.

Anatoli lit a cigarette and put it in Alexi's mouth while Alexi adjusted the drag. Clearly, to Jane, this big-fish catching was a matter of mind over muscle. The fish's strength weakened, proportional to the length of Alexi's cigarette. In the end a six-foot sturgeon languished beside the tug.

Anatoli gaffed the catch behind the gill. The captain gaffed it under the tail. They struggled to hold the river monster as it caught its second wind. It flopped and twisted, banging loudly against the side of the boat. Jane was startled when the struggle was interrupted by the throaty blast of a gun. Everybody starred as Vladimir holstered his still smoking sidearm. Blood bubbled from the sturgeon's head.

Dornish confronted Brutus.

"Pay up, asshole."

Brutus held his head high.

"If I wasn't so tired, I would..."

Dotz sided with his brother.

"But you are — so pay up."

Brutus grumbled as he counted out their winnings.

*****

As the sun set on the first evening Leonardo leaned on the bow rail with Madip.

"Fish was very tasty," he told Madip, in Russian.

"No. It much, much big. Much, much hard to chew," she answered, in broken Russian.

They watched the floodlight, cast from the wheelhouse, light the murky green water ahead of the boat.

"Keep eyes on river, Madip," the captain ordered, in Russian, as he panned the flood light that dimmed as he throttled down the engine.

Leonardo, a linguist, understood Madip's answer to mean:

"Don't worry. I seeing."

Then she told Leonardo the broken Russian equivalent of:

"I not trust that bully man, Vladimir."

"Neither do I."

"I scared of him. He look at me like tasty food."

In the ensuing conversation, Leonardo slowly bridged the language gap, learning the Shanyagir tribal tongue from Madip. He translated:

"I protect you," from Russian to Shanyagir.

"Vladimir want to…how to say? Him want to mate me."

"Ah, sex. Vladimir want sex – yes."

And so he learned the tribal words for *eat, protect,* and *sex.* Madip repeated:

"Vladimir want sex, me."

In time, Leonardo understood the pronoun translations for *you, me, him, her, them,* and *us.*

Then their conversation shifted to a topic of obvious importance to Madip.

"Valmpir want to eat us. I say to them. Captain listen. Jane hear – not listen," Madip distinguished by touching her ear and pointing, then the side of her head. "Others no hear. Leonardo hear?"

Leonardo gave her his inquisitive look.

"Valmpir?"

"Valmpir, mean people of Tunguska River…" she pantomimed, until Leonardo understood the word *valley.* "Tunguska River *valley people,* mean Valmpir in Shanyagir."

Leonardo gulped.

"Valmpir eat people?"

"Eat some. Make some like Valmpir."

"I'll make others listen to Madip."

Leonardo squeezed Madip's hand. To his surprise she squeezed his back. And it lingered…until Captain Bussie broke their spell.

"Look at river, Madip!"

CHAPTER 9

Leonardo woke, lying on the bow deck at dawn, with the help of a boot in his rib.

"Hey, what the hell…"

Vladimir leered down at him.

"Captain want girl."

Madip was asleep with her head on Leonardo's stomach. Leonardo shook her.

"Madip. Madip. Captain want you," he said in Shanyagir.

Vladimir's lip turned up at the edge.

"Sooo…you speak heathen language, now?"

Leonardo ignored him. Madip rubbed her eyes and yawned. When she saw Vladimir she jumped to her feet and straightened her coveralls. Leonard rose to stand between her and Vladimir. The captain called out from the aft side of the crew quarters.

"Madip!"

Madip ran off to her duties leaving Leonardo with Vladimir studying his face.

"You like skinny girl?" Vladimir asked slyly, in English.

Leonardo summoned up the most intimidating stare he could muster.

"My taste in women is none of your business."

Vladimir didn't blink.

"Vladimir ask – you answer."

The younger, smaller Leonardo tried his best to remain calm. Or at least not show any signs of fear.

"Or what?" Was the best answer he could come up with.
Vladimir laughed in his face.

"Listen boy. Vladimir see fear in your heart. And look – your leg is shaking."

Their standoff was interrupted by a cheerful and totally oblivious Sir Cedrick Falkner.

"Top of the morning, gentlemen."
Vladimir mumbled in Leonardo's ear.

"We continue our conversation later."
And then he walked away. Leonardo cleared his throat, wishing he could calm own his nerves.

"Why yes, Sir Cedrick. It is a lovely morning."

A commotion topped by Madip's voice took his attention. And he raced to her side.

"Nyet, Tunguska. Nyet, nyet, nyet."
Burling weighed in.

"It's a forty-mile hike through the forest, if we don't take that river."

"Madip refuses to go," Jane reasoned. "Do you expect us to drop her off at the fork?"

"Maybe," Burling answered.
A since of valor welled up in Leonardo's gut.

"Unacceptable. You can't just drop her off. She's been trying to warn you. Why aren't you listening? There are cannibals in the Tunguska River Valley."

"Are you still shaking, boy? Don't worry. Vladimir keep you safe."

Leonardo was pierced through the gut by Vladimir's outing. Cowardice, he thought he'd outlived, was about to murder his soul for the thousandth time. But Vladimir added salt to the wound.

"You want skinny girl? Be a man," Vladimir said, pounding his own chest.
Leonardo parried the insult, saying:

"For Christ's sake, man – this is not the time."

"That's right, boy – run to Jesus."
Leonardo was determined to conquer his own demons. And whatever the cost, he was about to lunge, when Madip astounded them all with a simple statement, in broken English.

"Jesus? Madip know Jesus."

Sir Cedrick broke the awkward pause.

"But you're just a heathen."

"Madip know Jesus," she insisted. "Jesus die for Madip bad. Jesus die for you bad. Madip know."

*****

And the angel, Pavilax, opened his earthly eyes to her.

CHAPTER 10

Pavilax, the guardian angel, collected his essence from heaven. And he formed, himself, as a misty cloud above the small boat carrying his charge. Madip looked like her mother, Kamen, whom he'd saved from the impact of the parasite baring comet that exploded over the Tunguska River twenty years earlier. He saved Kamen to protect the fetus – Madip.

Now, Pavilax admired the woman Madip had grown into. He looked down from on high, as twelve grumbled. Their leader took charge.
"Quiet. Everybody quiet. Go, or not go – is captain's decision."

Pavilax had intervened in earthly affairs on more occasions than the number hairs on a man's head. He understood power and war, greed, lust, and love. And many other things humans put before God. He understood every tongue spoken on the boat. And he understood the unspoken language of the heart.

They all looked at the large man as he pulled at his thick and graying beard. The one with a cunning heart, and a weapon hanging from his belt, passed the captain a flask of fermented drink.

After a long swig, the captain nodded.
"One hundred thousand rublis more."
The oldest man became animated.
"That wasn't part of the deal. We charted passage up the Angara and across the Tunguska."
"One hundred thousand, or you and your friends walk through forest."
"But, but…"

"Is settled," the captain said with finality, while the old man was still stuttering.

"But, but we don't have a hundred thousand rubles."

*****

Jane turned up her collar, looking up at the single cloud that hung low overhead; relieved that her and Burling's lives wouldn't be risked over Cedrick's obsession for space rocks. Her relief turned to shock when Vladimir yelled:

"I have hundred thousand rublis. We go!"

The captain laughed, heartily.

"Yes. We go!"

Jane's eyes met Madip's. Madip pulled her away from the ruckus, and into the galley.

*****

Madip remembered the sickening hiss of air rushing into her mother's skull, on the night a Valmpir broke open her head. Her mother, Kamen, had survived the initial wave of blood suckers. Those were *turned* by her brother, Chuchan, after he killed their brother, Chekan.

Kamen told Madip that Chuchan had eaten meat of an elk they'd slaughtered before the sky fell on the three of them. That was before Madip was born. Kamen's husband thought her crazy, but agreed to move to the far north. Madip thought her mother's story was fabricated to keep her from wandering away from their log house after dark.

And now Madip struggled, in her limited understanding of English, to recruit Jane for a mutiny.

"Madip no go," she said, pointing to herself.

Then she pointed to Jane.

"Jane no go. Jane go – Jane die. You man go – you man die. Madip no go."

Madip, frustrated by the blank look on Jane's face, sought a better way to explain. She got a melon out of a galley cabinet.

"Kamen - mother," she said pointing at the melon.

Jane obviously thought Madip was translating the word for melon; for she rubbed her belly and said.

"Ah yes, Kamen good."

England people slow in the brain. "Madip mother – Kamen."
   "Your mother eats Kamen?"

At wits end, Madip carved a face on the melon with a knife, and hung her own hair over the melon.
   "Kamen – Madip mother is Kamen."
Then she put the melon on the counter, and picked up a rolling pin.
   "Kamen," Madip repeated, holding the melon with her left hand.
   "Valmpir," she motioned with the rolling pin.

Madip bashed the melon with the rolling pin, broke it open with her hands…and sucked at the blue-green meat.

Jane threw up.

CHAPTER 11

They reached the inlet to the Tunguska River as the sun sat on the fifth day. Four were convicted not to turn onto the Tunguska. They huddled, whispering in the cleft of the bow.

"You must do something, Burling."

Leonardo agreed with Jane.

"You must convince Sir Cedrick that the risk is too high."

Madip's position was simple.

"Madip no go."

Heavy booted footsteps signaled his coming.

"You want mutiny?" Vladimir laughed, and patted the butt of his revolver. "Over Vladimir's dead body."

Madip squeezed in between Burling and Leonardo.

"Madip no go. Leonardo no go."

Vladimir shook his head, wagged his finger at Leonardo, and addressed Burling.

"Are you thinking to join in girly man's mutiny?"

Leonardo was glad that the girl he was growing quite fond of didn't know much English. But he couldn't live with himself if he didn't stand up. So up he stood. And he charged, intending to bury a shoulder in Vladimir's gut.

He awoke with his head in Madip's lap, wondering what happened.

"A knee to the face, young chap," Burling told him. "But at least you took a stand."

Leonardo checked himself for blood. *No blood.* But his head swam. And his right eye hurt something awful – before it closed, altogether.

"Be a lamb, Jane," Burling told his wife. "Get the boy some ice from the fish hold."

*****

Venus broke dusk, in the eastern sky, aft of the Perseyet. Captain Bussie completed his turn onto the Tunguska River and spun back the wheel. He told his first mate something, in Russian, and slid gracefully down the captain's ladder.

"Have never seen night so peaceful," he said, to no one in particular.

Burling and his wife overheard him.

"It is rather a peculiar calm, isn't it?"

Jane didn't answer.

"Jane – did you hear me?"

Jane cleared her throat.

"I have the strangest feeling that we're not supposed to be here."

"The captain agreed to wait here until morning. The girl said they only come out at night. We'll motor in at dawn, and be out before dusk."

The splash of anchors hitting the water calmed Janes nerves. Seeing Leonardo and Madip holding hands, Jane took Burling's hand.

"You'll owe me one hell of a shopping spree when this is all over."

Vladimir paced on the other side of the crew quarters. His footfalls were distinctive. *Maybe he won't come over here,* Jane thought. Eventually he did.

"Ahhh. Four lovers make good meal for night walkers."

This time, the captain himself intervened.

"Vladimir, for last time I tell you. Leave them alone, or I break your face."

The bagboys, Dornish and Dotz, snickered.

*****

Pavilax took an unseen hand off the small of the Captain's back, after the captain had done his bidding. His charge was safe – from Vladimir.

Madip took the first watch, just as she had done since Captain Bussie took her in, up in ice country. He'd lost a daughter her age, due to his own negligence, and felt fatherly affection towards Madip. He treated her like a daughter – unless he was drunk. And then she had to remind him that *she* was his second chance at being a good father. Lately, he was drunk more often.

The Perseyet sat motionless, on a river as smooth as glass. The captain ran her dark, and quiet, so as not to attract any attention from the wicked kind. Anatoli took over at midnight. Then Madip tucked herself away in her favorite place on earth – the bow cleft of the Perseyet.

Captain Bussie made his final rounds before turning in.
    "Stay frosty," he told the crew, in Russian.
Anatoli yawned and drank coffee from an hours old pot. He offered some to Leonardo, who lay backward in Madip's bosom. Leonardo declined. Anatoli took a few more gulps, sat the pot on the deck, and climbed the captain's ladder.

Madip whispered a prayer.
    "Jesus love us. Jesus come protect. Leonardo no die – Jesus.
She was about to doze off, when Vladimir stomped by, lighting his cigar with a pocket lighter. Madip shushed him. Vladimir ignored her.

*****

Silent, still, and all too peaceful was the night. A blanket of dead quiet hung over the dark forest. No owl hooted. No frog croaked. Not a single cricket chirped. Dead quiet is wicked. To reveal your presence is to die. This, Pavilax knew. And he rued the moment that Vladimir flicked his lighter.

The Tunguska River Valley food chain was contaminated with Satan's microbial parasites. At the top of that food chain were the *night stalkers* – two legged ravenous wolves that were once human. Their name struck fear in the hearts of every tongue.

They were the Valley People; called Valmpir and Beware-Wolves. And a band of them cocked heads towards Vladimir's lighter. They crept, naked and quiet, over the mossy forest floor. Then slinked, head first, into the water at the muddy river's edge. And slithered, breathless, along the silty riverbed – like eels. Pavilax nudged his charge and formed, unseen, as an invisible barrier between her and the things that climbed both anchor chains.

*****

Madip knew the Perseyet like a mother knows her unborn child. And she felt it list, ever so slightly, to starboard. She woke Leonardo with a soft hand over his mouth.

"Shhhhh."

She pulled him into the cleft, as far as they both could scooch.

"They coming," she whispered.

First, came a boney gray hand in the moonlight. Then a misshapen head, with hair like seaweed. If she screamed, her and Leonardo would die first. *Scream and die first. Not scream, and all others slaughtered in their sleep.*

The first Valmpir, with every rib visible, was on board. Another, bigger than the first, slung a webbed foot over the rail. Madip opened her mouth – for surely, she must sound a warning. *Where is Anatoli? Wake up. Please, wake up.*

The warning came from Leonardo; though he mispronounced it.

"Vampire! Vaaampire!"

*****

Both monstrosities lurched in their direction. And stopped, as if they'd hit wall of glass. Leonardo's stomach was in his throat. But he still had a moment to think it odd that the creatures pressed against…nothing at all.

Leonardo's warning was rewarded by a staccato of gunfire and a hail of flying lead.

"Ahhhhhh!" Vladimir roared along with his weapon, as muzzle flashes lit the night.

Leonardo had never even seen a machine gun. But he saw its issue pounding the smaller *thing* in the chest, until it flipped overboard. Wood chipped and flew as bullets bit into the Perseyet. When the shooting stopped, Vladimir yelled at the second *thing*.

"I knew you would come. Vladimir call – you come!"

Screams of panic and pain came from aft of the crew compartment. Then two loud splashes. Leonardo had no time to process.

The second Valmpir had holes in it. Leonardo could see smoke coming out of them. But it acted as if it hadn't been touched. Vladimir pounded a fist on the side his machine gun. It was jammed. He threw it on the deck. It went off as he drew his side arm. The volley pushed the machine gun toward Leonardo, as Vladimir emptied his revolver into the juggernaut.

"Pick it up!" Vladimir yelled in Leonardo's direction.

And Leonardo tried, but there was a wall of nothing in the way.

"Pick it up, you coward! Pick it up!

The night-stalker snatched Vladimir up and shook him in the air like a rag doll. Try as he might, Leonardo couldn't get to the fallen weapon. Vladimir let out a death scream, as the thing sank teeth into his neck.

CHAPTER 12

A thunder clap from Burling's hunting rifle took the head off the mutant that held Vladimir. Both fell to the ground.

"Lights!" Captain Busies voice rang out, in Russian. "Lights, Alexi. Lights."

*****

A gas-powered generator sputtered to life. The warm glow of the spotlight brightened to full beam, revealing the carnage on the bow. The deck was awash with blood. Burling Payne stood over the two bodies, pointing his long rifle at the chest of the headless one.

Pavilax held his ground until Madip and Leonardo got up. Blood oozed into the cleft after he let them pass. Madid grabbed a gaff from its perch, as lanterns blossomed in light.

"No touch blood. No touch."

"Here – let me," Leonardo told her and took the gaff.

The captain grabbed another, and Alexi a third. The three of them muscled the headless hulk over the side. Leonardo reached for the machine gun, but Madip cautioned him:

"No Touch."

It was covered in blood.

A woman's scream, two small caliber shots, and another splash sent Burling running.

"Jaaaaane!"

Leonardo cleared the crew cabin just in time to see Burling drop his rifle and jump in after his wife. Captain Bussie wailed, in Russian.

"Anatoli! Start engine!"

No answer came.

"Do you hear me, Anatoli? Start boat!"

"Him dead!" Madip yelled back.

Dotz cried out to his brother, Dornish.

"Dornish! Swim Dornish! Noooo…"

Leonard ran back to find Madip climbing the ladder to the helm, where Anatoli was slumped over the wheel. He tracked bullet holes up the wall, with his eyes, surmising that Anatoli had been shot when Vladimir dropped his machine gun on the deck. *Two shot dead. Three in the water.*

"Up anchors," Madip shouted.

The engine cranked three times before it chugged to a start. Leonardo cranked the handle on the bow anchor chain wheel, while watching Brutus crank the aft anchor.

Jane screamed from the water.

"Heeeelp!" She gurgled. "Heeeelp."

The captain hauled her in, over the starboard rail, and yelled in Russian.

"Get us away from here, Madip!"

His intent was clear.

"No! Wait!" Jane coughed. "Burling's still out there."

The captain pointed the aft spot light toward the shore. A gray and naked man-thing dragged Burling's limp body onto the river bank.

"He's there." Jane yelled, over the deep throated engine. "We have to go get him."

"Nyet!" The captain ordered. "Madip. Go!"

Leonardo felt the boat shudder when Madip put her in reverse. She gunned the throttle, churning up diesel vapor and water, aft of the Perseyet. In spite of her efforts, the boat only moved closer to the river bank. Madip pointed the bow light to shore.

"Look!" She pointed. "Valmpir!"

A pack of them dragged the bow anchor up the river bank and waged a tug-of-war with the Perseyet. Another pack was tearing a dead body apart by its limbs.

"Dooornish! Dotz screamed. "Oh God – noooo."

"Move aside!" Jane warned, shouldering her husband's hunting rifle."

Ka-woom! A perfect headshot dropped the beast that dragged Burling.

"Somebody, go get him," Jane pleaded.

Captain Bussie overruled her plea.

"Nyet! Madip, go!"

"No!" Jane cycled the bolt and took aim at the pack pulling the anchor.

"Not without my husband."

Ka-woom! One fell over, but three took its place.

Brutus wound the aft anchor into its nest.

"Go, Madip. Go, go, go."

Jane cycled the bolt again. But this time she aimed at the captain's chest.

"Go and get him."

Burling was stirring on all fours. The captain raised his hands.

"I not going."

Jane looked to Brutus, Alexi, and Dotz. No one volunteered. But Dotz cried.

"He was the *brave* one. They should have taken *me*."

The Perseyet was losing ground to the ever-growing hoard of Valley People.

"Isn't there a man among you?" Jane sobbed. "Pleeease, for the love of God. Someone get him."

Leonardo pondered his own fate. Then he dove in head first; wishing he hadn't, before he even hit the water. Madip screamed.

"Leonardo, noooooo!"

*****

To protect his charge, Pavilax lent angelic strength to the cause of the Perseyet, dragging a gaggle of zombies into the water. The captain ran to the forward anchor chain with bolt cutters. The chain broke just as Leonardo reached Burling.

"Come on, man. We have to swim for it. I'll help you, but we have to go - NOW!"

The pack all fell when the anchor chain gave way. But when they rose, they turned on Leonardo and Burling.

"Leonardo, ruuuun!" Madip yelled.

*****

No more running. Leonardo was determined not to leave Burling alone. And he turned to meet death head on. At the last moment, he closed his eyes, and prepared for wicked, grizzly death.

CHAPTER 13

A deafening hail of machine gun fire jolted Leonardo's eyes open. Bullets tore into gray flesh with sickening thuds. When the shooting stopped, Vladimir wailed.

"You want more? Vladimir give you more!"

Leonardo helped Burling into the water, hoping that Vladimir was reloading. He didn't hope for long. Vladimir unleashed what must have been another hundred rounds into everything standing.

Leonardo was nearly out of strength as he dragged Burling through cold water. *We're both going to drown.*

As he looked up at Madip, for what was sure to be the last time, she spun the wheel. The bow swung round to meet the men in the water. Vladimir emptied another magazine while they were dragged aboard.

Leonardo felt the kick when Madip shifted gears. And they sped off into the night. He lie soaked on his back, looking up at the stars as he caught his breath. Familiar footfalls approached, unseen. A hand reached down to grab his.

"I was wrong about you. Was bravest thing Vladimir has ever seen."

Vladimir's clothes were covered in blood.

CHAPTER 14

Los Angeles, CA.
Monday, 17 January 2000

A young couple walked briskly along a crowded Westwood Boulevard, just off the campus of UCLA. The strawberry-blonde woman, Cortney Landau, stood five-feet-eight in her bare feet. Presently she wore three-inch platform knee high boots over leggings.

"Hurry up, Stocker it's freezing out here."

"You're from the East Coast," the six-foot tall man answered. "You can't possibly think this is cold."

"My blood has thinned; okay?"

Stocker held the door of the "Campus Roast" coffee shop, known affectionately to a nerdy bunch as 'Hackers' Café.

"After you, Cortney."

Three of their fellow students waved for their attention from a table in the corner of the crowded establishment. Laptop computers were open on a dozen tables.

Stocker led Cortney through the lunch crowd..

"Excuse me. Oops – sorry. Comin' through."

Cortney smiled at the trio hunched behind a single laptop screen.

"Dungeons and Dragons today, boys?"

"Nope," the mop top redhead at the keyboard, Brice, answered. "But pull up a chair."

Stocker looked around for a fifth chair.

"Is this chair taken?" He asked a sheepish looking kid at a nearby table.

Cortney felt a little awkward when Stocker held the chair for her. *When did we stop being just friends?*

"You didn't have to do that," she whispered as she sat.

Trevor, who sat to Brice's right, must have noticed something fishy too.

"It's never gonna happen, Stocker."

He's making it worse. Please just let it go.

"Okay so what are you geeks up to now?"

"Oh, come on guys; really?" Stocker whined over Cortney's shoulder.

Cortney looked up at him.

"What? What's wrong?"

He didn't answer her, but admonished the nerdy trio.

"Man, you can't have that sitting in plain view like that."

The third kid, nicknamed 'Gizmo', put his coat over a little black box that was connected to the laptop.

"Oh, right – sorry."

Cortney hadn't even noticed it.

"Why? what is it?"

"It's a digital sniffer."

Now she was curious and scooted her chair around the table.

"What does it do?"

Stocker shook his head and took a seat opposite the laptop.

"It's an RF transceiver mod/demod."

"A *what?*"

"Modulator, Demodul…"

"I'm a microbiology major. I'm not stupid. Just explain it in English."

Stocker shook his head slowly.

"They're hacking from a distance," he explained.

"Where's the other end plugged in?"

"Shhh. It's behind a plant, in the Registrar's Office," Gizmo whispered with a broad smile.

Trevor pointed at the screen.

"Open that tab, right there."

"Shut up, dweeb," Brice snickered. "I know how to drive."

Cortney was taken aback at what she saw on the screen.

"Hey those are our Art Appreciation grades from last semester."

Brice shushed her.

"Yeah, I know. But I needed a 'B' in that class."

He used the finger pad to move the cursor to the grade beside his grade. With the tap of his finger he said:

"There," and changed his 'C' to a 'B'.

Cortney protested aloud.

"You can't do that!"
After the four boys shot her a warning stare, she whispered.
"Put it back!"
Brice moved the cursor to Cortney Landau's name.
"Nope," he said with a straight face.
And with a keystroke he changed her grade from a 'B' to an 'A'.

Cortney glared at Brice.
"You're gonna get us all expelled, you idiot."
Stocker glanced out the window.
"Oh snap! It's Professor Stanton. Unplug the sniffer."
Cortney felt their urgency.
"Who's Professor Stanton?"
Gizmo answered, as the screen jumbled to an error screen.
"He's our Digital Surveillance instructor. Act normal."
Cortney was fit to be tied.
"Act normal? I've got nothing to do with this. You change that back as soon as he leaves," she whispered.

The waitress came to their table. The boys pointed to their coffees and declined to order anything else. The waitress popped her gum and looked at Stocker.
"Oh, um. Two coffees – room for cream."
He looked at Cortney.
"And two bear claws."
So now he's ordering for me. "Make mine a cheese Danish, please."
Then she looked across the table at Stocker.
"Why do you hang around with these goofballs anyway?"
"The ugly one in the middle is my cousin," Stocker laughed.
Cortney looked from Stocker's neatly coifed brown hair, to Brice's shaggy red hair, and back again.
"By marriage," Brice added, sarcastically.

Cortney moved her chair back to Stocker's side of the table and pulled a small bible from her coat pocket.
"Can I read you guys a few verses?"
Her request was met with groans.
"Do we have to?"
"Not that again."
"Come on Stocker," Brice pleaded, "Tell your girl…"
"Look," Cortney insisted. "I've sat through your hacker chat and Dungeons and Dragons for a whole semester. Indulge me for a few minutes."

"Oh look at the time," Brice mocked and packed up his laptop, and Gizmo's gizmo, and put them in his backpack.

Stocker pleaded Cortney's case.
"Come on man; give it a chance."
"Not a chance," Brice said and headed for the door.
Cortney shook a finger at him as he left the table, and snapped:
"You change that back."

Courtney held out both hands.
"Come on," she said to the rest. "Take hands. We'll start with a prayer."
The boys reluctantly held hands.
"God, please be with us as we dive into your word…"
Stocker interrupted.
"How bout we just dip our toe, for now?"

Cortney turned to 'The Gospel of John,' and read:
"In the beginning was the Word, and the Word was *with* God, and the Word *was* God. He was in the beginning with God. All things were made through Him, and without Him nothing was made that was made. In Him was life, and the life was the light of men. And the light shines in the darkness, and the darkness did not comprehend it…"

Gizmo squirmed in his chair, as Cortney read.
"…And the Word became flesh and dwelt among us."
Cortney didn't want to run him off.
"Okay; thank you both for indulging me. Besides, I gotta get some rest. I had to take a night class – first night."

Gizmo and Stocker looked back and forth at one another.
"Which class?" Gizmo asked.
"Political Science. I needed it to graduate on time. Fun, right?"
"Uh oh."
"Uh oh, what?"
Trevor pursed his lips.
"Steer clear of that weird Asian girl."
"What? Half the campus is Asian."
Gizmo clarified.
"That's racist, Bro. She's Japanese; not Chinese, not Korean, not Vietnamese, not…"
Courtney cut him off.
"Okay I get it, Gizmo. But how is she weird?"
Trevor shook his head.

"You haven't seen her."

"He's right Cortney," Stocker said and reached for her hand. "I've heard stories."

Cortney pulled her hands out of his reach.

I wish he'd stop that. "Stories? What kind of stories?"

"Forget the stories," Trevor intruded into Stocker's clumsy attempt at chivalry. "She looks dead. No one ever sees her in the daytime. And she drinks blood out of a…"

"Get out."

"I swear, Cortney. Mitch saw it drip down her chin."

"OoKaaaay – what's her name?"

"Karen something. She's a vampire for sure. Stay away from her."

CHAPTER 15

A gaunt looking girl, of Asian descent, sat in the back row of Professor Richter's 7:30pm Political Science class, as he presented foundational terms.
"Communism, Socialism, Totalitarianism…"

Cortney tuned him out and turned to peek at the girl she surmised was Karen. And leaning over to her friend, Selena, she whispered,
"Is that her?"

Selena was blonde, by Clairol, with slightly Hispanic features.
"Shhhh. Yes, that's her."
The next time Cortney looked back, Karen was already staring back at her. *Oh crap; she sees me.*

Cortney went out of her way to keep her eyes on the professor as he droned on.
"…Now let's look at Democracy – power of the people, by the people, and for the people…."
Cortney wasn't listening. Her mind was on the weird Japanese girl in the back corner of the room. She had to sneak another peek.

Karen wasn't paying attention either. When Cortney turned around, Karen was still staring at her.
"Salena, she's staring at me."
"Well stop looking, stupid."
"She's so tiny…"
"Shhh."

*****

Karen Okawa walked alone after class. She arrived home, after an unplanned encounter with a male student, and made a satellite phone call to Eastern Belarus. An impatient Nadia Roman answered in Russian.

"*Doklad.*"

"Doklad. Ya nenevizhu eto…."

"*You don't have to like it, Karen….*"

"I didn't say I disliked it. I said I hated it."

"*No matter. Are you healthy?*"

"You could have sent anyone, Nadia. Why me?"

"*I'm not sure I understand your tone.*"

"Sozhaleyu."

"*Don't be sorry. Be effective. I sent you because you fit in, there. Now tell me — are you well?*"

"I only have three pellets left."

"*Don't worry. We are ahead of schedule. ARE YOU WELL?*"

"Yes."

"*And how is the weather there in California?*"

"Cold enough."

"*Good, Karen. Have you been behaving yourself?*"

"Yes."

"*Kaaaren?*"

"Yes. I told you — yes."

"*Do you expect me to believe you've been there two whole months without….*"

"The why did you ask?"

"*Just cover your tracks!*"

The red light on Karen's sat-phone told her that her boss had hung up.

"Cover your tracks," she mocked, as she pulled off her bloody sweatshirt.

CHAPTER 16

Washington, DC.
Tuesday, 18 January 2000

Gary Landau awakened five minutes ahead of the alarm. Instinctively, he reached over for his wife. *Not there?* His gut wrenched. She'd been gone for over a month. His protective instinct flailed like a detached umbilical cord. His daughter hadn't called since she flew back to college. *Call Cortney.* Extracting himself from a fortress of pillows, he stumbled from his bed and did a mental coin-toss. *Cortney or coffee. Coffee or Cortney.* After two unanswered calls, he headed for the coffee pot.

After a shower, shave, and other biologics, Gary stood bewildered in his closet. No more were there perfectly pressed shirts and pants. Neither would the pantry be full when he got there.

Gary tied his shoes, put on rubber pullovers, and donned his wool coat over his least wrinkled clothes. The Washington D.C. winter bit him in the face when he stepped outside. Rather than scrape ice from the car windows, he made a conscious decision to be late for work. He started up his late model Chrysler and let the engine idle while the windows defrosted.

While he waited, he wondered if his wife, Kathrin, would come back home. She hadn't gotten her own place yet. He missed the old days; back when he made a real difference. *I can make a jet dance on its tail, but I can't even dress myself. Pathetic.*

A traffic jam on K Street added to his tardiness. There were no more empty parking spaces in the John Adams building parking lot where he worked.

He raced another driver for an empty parking space in the Madison Street parking lot. He lost. Blowing his horn at the winner only added to his own frustration. *Who'd of ever thought it? Gary Landau – a librarian.*

Back up lights came on, on the hind-side of a late model BMW. Gary was patient for the first thirty seconds. *Must be a woman fixing her makeup.* In another thirty seconds he was tooting his horn. *Now she's gonna move even slower.* He leaned on the horn and the car finally inched backward. The BMW driver locked eyes with Gary as she backed out. *Oh that's just great.* Of all the people to see him coming in late. The lady driver was his new boss, Judy Haynsworth.

The Library of Congress loomed large over the snow-covered campus. Gary decided that none of his coworkers needed to see him coming in forty-five minutes late. He cut through the Thomas Jefferson building, to go in the side entrance of the John Adams building.

At five-foot-ten, the top of Gary's graying blonde head was even with the partitions as he slinked to his cubicle. Jefferson Hicks was six-three, and sported a well-coiffed afro that Gary spotted in *his* office.

Jeff spoke with a commanding basso-profundo that rattled the chests of anyone in earshot.
    "Oh hey, Gary. I was just leaving you a note. Judy came by here lookin for you, bout fifteen minutes ago. I told her you were probably in the 'john'."
    "Nice try, Jeff. But I ran into her in the parking lot; rather unceremoniously. Have a seat if you want."

Gary hung his coat on a partition hook and sat in his swivel chair to take off his rubber over shoes. Jeff didn't sit.
    "Somethings up. Judy called an all hands in the classified conference room. Eleven hundred hours. She just left for a briefing at the Pentagon."

Gary nodded, knowing he couldn't talk about it in his unclassified office area. He made a coded hand gesture; a twirl of the finger, that silently asked Jeff, 'What time-zone?'

Jeff held up seven fingers, which meant seven hours ahead of D.C. *The Baltics.*
    "And, Gary?"
    "Yeah?"
    "I know you don't like this job, but you're flushing my credibility down

the toilet with yours."

"Shhh," Gary shushed him. "How come you never learned to whisper. You know I'm grateful. If it weren't for you, I'd still be home rotting away. It's just that – don't you miss being important?"

Jeff shook his head.

"I was never important, Gary. *You* were the top-gun fighter pilot. I was just your crew chief. Eleven o'clock, Gary. Don't be late."

CHAPTER 17

Judy Haynsworth was on her feet, in the middle of her introduction, when Gary walked into the secret conference room five minutes late.

"Sorry," he said quietly. Judy continued, but followed Gary with her eyes as he climbed awkwardly over several people to find an empty seat. *Way to go, Gary.*

"Now let's get down to business. There is a situation currently unfolding in the Baltics. Belarus, to be exact." She paused thoughtfully and looked around the room. "Is everyone here cleared?"

Everyone looked around, but no one acknowledged lacking a security clearance. She went on.

"The Joint Chiefs of Staff were called into an emergency session by the Secretary of Defense last night. The Secretary briefed me this morning. Our intelligence sources tell us that the Belarussian government has misplaced a convoy of SS-25 Road-Mobile Missile Launchers."

The listeners became vocal, carrying on several disjointed conversations.

"Let's have one meeting please! Let me give you the details, then we'll open it up for discussion. The Belarussians are admitting to not knowing the whereabouts of ten mobile missile launchers. We think the actual number is at least twice that. The launchers were on the way to Kostroma, to be decommissioned and disassembled in accordance with the START-II Treaty. The convoy left Vyetka, Belarus, en route for Kostroma; a trip of about five hundred miles, yesterday at oh-four-hundred hours their time."

"What's the time difference?" Someone murmured.

"They're eight hours ahead of us," another responded.

"Seven hours," several corrected in unison.

Judy continued.

"Our intelligence on the ground confirmed that the convoy left the base. They said they thought there weren't supposed to be any missiles. As soon as Space Command heard that there *were* missiles..."

"Missiles? There haven't been any nukes in Belarus since ninety-six!" A senior member of the staff blurted out, insinuating that Judy must have gotten the facts twisted.

"Make that ninety-seven," Gary corrected. "Those missiles shouldn't have nuclear warheads."

"As I was saying," Judy cut back in, "as soon as Space Command heard that there were missiles, they moved a satellite over the area to look for beta particles. But there's a blind spot under the Chernobyl fallout region.

We had visual satellite surveillance over the area by oh-seven-fifteen — forty-five minutes after sunup and... no sign of them. They couldn't have gotten more than two hundred miles or so. When pressed, the Belarussians admitted losing the launchers. They're still denying the loss of any missiles. NORAD has gone to DEFCON Four. The Secretary needs all the background we can give him. We'll be working late this week, so clear your calendars. I'll take questions now."

Judy took a seat at the head of the large conference table. Gary's hand shot up, but he didn't wait to be acknowledged.

"Were the launchers version A or B?" He asked, with a concern not understood by most of the people in the room.

Judy thumbed through the file labeled "Belarus" and found the reference.

"Version B. Why do you ask?"

"Because the B's can be maintained and operated by a much smaller crew. *And* they've been upgraded to accommodate a remote wide area network. That means that as few as, say...forty people could ready and launch all twenty missiles. They'd be the perfect terrorist weapon if they had warheads. And by the way, an SS-25 launched from Belarus could put a five-megaton warhead anywhere on the planet."

"I see," Judy said.

Gary went on.

"So, did they have warheads?"

Judy nodded.

"Yes."

"How many did our operative see?"

"More than he could count. All of the launchers carried missiles, and all the missiles had warheads. There were other trucks carrying them too."

"How in God's name could we let that happen?" Gary prodded.

"They didn't have the time, or the expertise, to dismantle them in

Vyetka."

"Excuse me," Jeff's voice vibrated the big mahogany table. "But that convoy was scheduled to go out next month."

"That's right. But it was pushed ahead on short notice to decrease the probability of this very situation," Judy explained.

"Had to be an inside job," Jeff added. "Any idea who did it?"

"That's part of our charter," Judy replied, inferring that the Russian Studies Division might actually find the answer.

A petite woman of Asian descent held up a finger. Judy gave a nod in her direction.

"I'm Anne Li," she began.

"You maintain the satellite imagery data base, right?" Judy asked.

"That's right. I was wondering, just how large is the Chernobyl fallout region?"
Judy went back to the file.

"Over a hundred and sixty thousand square kilometers total, in northern Ukraine and southeastern Belarus."

"As I recall from a satellite image that I filed some time ago, the worst of the fallout zone stretches about a hundred miles to the northeast of Vyetka. It seems more than just a coincidence that the missiles were snatched in that area."

"Good point. I'm sure the CIA is aware of it," Judy said, jotting a note in the file.

"Wait a minute," Gary interjected. "The Chernobyl accident released a hundred times more radiation than the bomb dropped on Hiroshima. The region just northeast of Vyetka is a radioactive desert. It's the largest hot spot outside of Chernobyl itself. The entire region was confiscated by the government and fenced off, with a couple dozen other keep-out zones. There's over forty curies of radiation per square kilometer there. And Cesium 137 is nasty stuff. It loves to get into tree roots, soil, ground water and..."

"Gary," Judy interrupted. "can we save the detailed technical discussion for later?"

"I'm trying to make a point!" Gary pushed on. "What I'm trying to say is that only a complete lunatic would be using that nuclear wasteland for cover. A person would exceed a year's safe dosage in a matter of hours."

"Alright then. Thank you for the analysis. Here are some of the things I think we'll need to pull together," Judy said, bringing an abrupt end to the open forum. "We'll need detailed maps. Jim," she said, looking at a young man in his late twenties, "you'll handle that."
The man nodded.

"Anne will, of course, provide satellite imagery and photographs. Gary, we'll need all the technical information you can get us on the weapons systems and their current configuration – and of course, your written assessment of the fallout situation. Jeff can work with you. My direct staff will work the socio-political angle. Let's see – what are we missing?"

"I'll work local and international news," a woman named Irene volunteered.

"We'll need a couple of people to cover congress," a bearded man sitting next to Jeff, added.

"Who usually covers congressional committee meetings?" Judy asked. Three hands shot up.

"Okay, you guys have it. There'll be special sessions all week. Are you getting all this?" Judy asked her secretary.
The secretary nodded and kept writing.

"Passports," came a voice over her shoulder.
Judy turned to see who was speaking.

"Your name is?"

"Pat, ma'am," said an unassuming yet intense fellow. "It is not unreasonable to assume that our government may want to send in a diplomatic team; some of ourselves included."

"I hadn't considered that," Judy told him.

"I'll put together a list of candidates, if you like," Pat offered.

"A tentative list," Judy said begrudgingly.
When Jeff asked, "Do you think the CIA will let us in bed with them on the terrorist angle?" debate broke out all over the room.

This was the sorest of subjects. The CIA despised the library researchers. They were considered amateurs; nerdy bookworms who never actually got their hands dirty. The librarians, on the other hand, were always trying to change their image by constantly volunteering to help in the trenches.

"Alright, alright!" Judy shouted. "Here's what we'll do. We'll gather all the information we can about suspect terrorist organizations. But we'll do it quietly, and we'll use benign sources only. No informants. No stepping on any agency toes. Is that clear?"

All heads nodded in agreement.

"We'll share our findings when we've got a comprehensive package. Now – discussions on any other matters would be a bit anti-climactic. So let's get to work. I'll expect status reports tomorrow at three, in this room. Thank you."

Judy stood up, looked at her watch, and without another word she left the room.

CHAPTER 18

Gary combed through every file containing information about the SS-25 Sickle Intercontinental Ballistic Missiles and the version B mobile launchers. So far, he found nothing that he didn't already know, or have access to in his personal files back in his office. He sat at a computer workstation in the Science Reading Room on the south side of the Adam's Building's fifth floor. He'd spent two hours searching the automated bibliographic database. This was all public domain stuff. He had to go deeper.

"You getting anywhere?" He whispered to Jeff who was sitting at the next station.

"Not really. How bout you?" Jeff's voice boomed, even though he was trying to whisper.

"You can find any of this stuff in Aviation Week, we're gonna have to go behind the wall," Gary said, rubbing his temple.

"We can't go…"

"Shhh. Keep it down."

"We can't go in the closed area. They'll see us as soon as we log on," Jeff said in an all-out attempt at a whisper.

"Come on, we can talk in that reading room," Gary said, pointing to an open door.

The librarians strolled casually across the reading room. Senator Bowen looked up from the journal he was reading. He knew Jeff and Gary, and they exchanged greetings as they passed.

"What're you boys up to?" The senator asked, with narrowed eyes and a southern accent.

The pair didn't answer, but continued past the Computer Catalog Center and out into an empty reading room.

"Are you nuts, Gary?" Jeff bellowed. "You know what happened the last time we accessed classified weapons files. They were all over us in ten minutes. We spent a whole month justifying our actions, and that time we didn't have specific orders to stay out!"

"Jeff, you know better than anybody that if orders and right get into a scrap in my yard, I'm gonna help right come out on top. For cryin out loud — it's not like we don't have need-to-know!"

Jeff nodded slowly.

"They're still gonna see us."

"Maybe not. We just need to be careful with our keyword search. We'll use something that doesn't raise a flag."

"Like what?"

"I don't know." Gary said, while pacing.

"Parade," Jeff said succinctly.

"That's it! The Russian nations always show off their weapons on parade. Let's get to it."

*****

Jeff opened file after file on a secret computer while he and Gary poured over the pictures of past Belarussian parades and the associated text. Jeff leaned back and stretched.

"We're all the way back to nineteen ninety-three and we haven't seen anything so far that we didn't already know."

"Yeah, I know, but there has to be something. Think we ought to split up so we can cover more ground?" Gary asked.

"I still think four eyes are better than two. Let's keep going."

"Yeah, I agree. Let's go in the other direction and just concentrate on the photos."

"Back to ninety-four?"

"Yeah, ninety-four."

Jeff opened the folder corresponding to 1994. He zoomed in on every marking, on every missile, and every launcher pictured. After several dozen photos he opened the folder labeled 1995.

"I wonder if either of the other teams is having any better luck . . ."

"Hold on," Gary said. "There was something in that last batch. Go back for a minute."

Jeff reopened the previous folder. On the second photo Gary sang out.

"That's the one, right there!" Gary pointed to the screen. "Zoom in on the crowd next to the launcher."

Jeff doubled the size of the shot.

"Recognize anybody?" Gary asked with a widening smile.

"Hard to tell in the half-light. Must be late in the evening. Well, I'll be damned. That's Markov Gregor. I thought he died at Chernobyl."

"So did I. Open another file."

A few mouse clicks displayed the next photo.

"Well I'll be damned. There he is again!"

"Sure is," Jeff agreed. "We've been so busy looking at hardware that we ignored the crowd. Looks like he's walking beside the launcher."

"They both are," Gary said, pointing to a statuesque brunette pictured beside Markov.

Jeff opened three more photos from the ninety-four parade. Gregor and the tall dark- haired woman were in every one of them that were taken after sunset.

"You know …I've seen her before," Jeff said slowly.

"Where?"

"Let me think about it for a minute."

Jeff stood up and paced with a thumb to his chin.

"It was last year, I think. Where was it . . .?"

After a moment, Jeff snapped his finger.

"Got it! Last summer when the Belarussian Minister of the Interior was assassinated. The wire services covered excerpts from his final speech. Gary, that woman was part of the minister's entourage."

"Are you sure?"

"You don't forget a face like that. Especially when it's standing beside a pudgy politician. Yeah, I'm sure. And it'll be easy enough to verify."

"Alright. Let's assume you're right, Jeff. That puts a resurrected Soviet nuclear physicist in the same company as an assassinated Belarussian politician. And we're not talking just any Soviet physicist; Markov Gregor designed those warheads all by himself. We have to assume they're operational. "

"So we've got missing launchers, and missiles, with an underground scientist who has the smarts to arm the warheads," Jeff summarized.

"Well that gets the hard part out of the way. We're also talking about a woman having ties to a government that just lost a couple dozen armed ICBM's."

Gary and Jeff looked at each other.

"We gotta find out who she is," Jeff said.

"And *where* she is," Gary added. "Come on, log off. We're too easy to trace in here."

"I thought I already told you that?"

"Yeah – I gotta make a phone call anyway."

Gary took his mobile phone off the shelf, outside the skiff, and speed-dialed his daughter's phone.

"Hello."

"Hey Cortney."

"Hi dad."

"How come you didn't call when you landed?"

"I'm sorry. I called mom. Didn't she tell you?"

"Your mom and I don't speak much these days."

"I wish you two would keep me out of your drama."

"Sorry. I just wanted to know you're safe. Sorry to bother you."

"I'm safe, Dad."

"I love you Cortney."

"I love you too, Dad...bye."

"Bye."

"She still mad at you, Gary?"

"Still mad."

"Give it time, ole buddy. Give it time. It's 8:30. Let's call it a night."

CHAPTER 19

Mitch Pascara, a second degree Taekwondo blackbelt, practiced a Kata in his empty dojo. Cortney, wearing a black wool coat over her gi, bowed in. Mitch acknowledged her with a quick nod, without breaking his rhythm. Cortney took off her coat and boots and wrapped a stiff brown belt twice round her waist.

Mitch spun in a full circle with a face high, spinning heel kick, followed by a full circle, ankle high sweep. *How the heck does he do that*, Cortney thought as she cinched her belt with a perfect knot.

Mitch shot a gut level side kick and held it while he greeted Cortney.
  "Haven't seen you since I promoted you."
  "Home for the holidays, Mitch."
  "It's only five-thirty. Why so early?"
  "I needed to talk to you in private."
  "Hold on."

Cortney stretched while Mitch completed his kata.
  "Ok Cortney, what's up?"
  "You're not even breathing hard."
  "Conditioning. It's what you get when you don't take time off."
  "I'll be here every class. But you gotta teach me to sweep."
Mitch nodded.
  "Let's stretch while we talk. I don't wanna cool off."
Cortney mirrored Mitch's stretch routine.
  "Selena says you know that Japanese girl in my night class."
  "She's not Japanese. She's Russian."
  "How is she Russian?"

"Her Japanese father married her Russian mother, in Russia. Stay away from her."

"Why? She's just an itty-bitty thing."

"Cortney, believe me, you don't even want that girl to know your name. Just stay away from her."

"Oops. I think I already got her attention. But what's the big deal?"

Mitch stopped in the middle of a side stretch.

"Remember Godfrey?"

"That big Black guy you called Sasquatch?"

"Yeah, that guy. Did you ever wonder why he stopped coming to class?"

"Noooo...not really. But why?"

Mitch wiped sweat from his brow with the sleeve of his gi.

"I kicked him out for being too aggressive. I warned him twice. Anyway, let me tell you what I saw one night in the village with my own eyes.

Karen Okawa was sitting outside of Starbucks minding her own business. Just staring off into space. The guys at the table with Godfrey were getting pretty loud – talking about *her*. Godfrey wasn't really in on it. He was just laughing. When the guys stood up to leave, Karen got up and blocked their path. I was about to get up, cause I knew things were about to get out of hand."

Mitch talked with his hands moving.

""She didn't even come up to Godfrey's chest. I guess she picked him, cause he was the biggest. She's holding a Starbucks cup in her hand.

"What's so funny?" She says to Godfrey.

And Godfrey even apologized; which blew me away cause he's such a jerk...""

"Mitch!"

"What?"

"Can you please get to the point?"

Mitch smiled, and joked:

"Good thing you're my friend. She dropped her cup and punched Godfrey with her palm. Right there." He said, touching Cortney's solar plexus.

"She caught the cup before it hit the ground. But..."

"But what?"

"Blood spilled out of that little hole in the top."

"Come on," Cortney chided.

"I saw it with my own eyes. After the cops left, I *touched* it."

"Cops?"

"She almost killed Godfrey. They had to give him CPR. He didn't wake up until the cops got there. And he wasn't about to tell them that he got

KO'd by a skinny, five-foot tall girl."

I shouldn't have looked at her. Selena told me not to look at her. "When did all this happen?"

"You must'a been on vacation. Just stay away from her. Got it?"

Cortney's phone played a ditty.

"Come on, Cortney – no phones in the dojo."

"Sorry, Mitch."

Cortney bowed out and answered.

"Hello."

"Hey Cortney."

"Hi dad."

"How come you didn't call when you landed?"

"I'm sorry. I called mom. Didn't she tell you?"

"Your mom and I don't speak much these days."

"I wish you two would keep me out of your drama."

"Sorry. I just wanted to know you're safe. Sorry to bother you."

"I'm safe, Dad."

"I love you Cortney."

"I love you too, Dad…bye."

"Bye."

She left the phone, shaking her head.

"Ok, Mitch. Now teach me that sweep."

CHAPTER 20

Los Angeles, Ca.
Wednesday, 19 January 2000

Cortney rushed in on the lunch crowd at *Hacker's* Café. She danced passed two paramedics leaving in a hurry.

"Hey!" She snapped as she came up behind Trevor and gizmo with their noses buried in a laptop screen.

Gizmo sat straight up, with a start. Trevor slammed the laptop shut.

"Sheesh, Cortney, you almost gave me a heart attack. You can't just sneak up on us like that."
Gizmo was about to add his two cents.

"You scared the b'Jesus out of..."

"Nevermind that," she interrupted. "Where's Brice?"

"Haven't seen him since the other day," Trevor admitted. "Stocker was just in here looking for him. Why? What's up?"

"My friend, Selena just told me she saw him walking with Creepy Karen, Monday night after class."
Gizmo laughed.

"Yeah, he's intrigued by her dark, *Goth* persona."

"We have to warn him," Cortney insisted.

"Hold on there, sister. Nerds need love too. And if Creepy Karen is the best he can do..."
Cortney found nothing funny.

"Shut your filthy mouth, Gizmo. That girl's bad news. We have to find him."

Cortney was punched in the gut by the abrupt blare of a nearby siren. An ambulance eased out of the cramped parking lot; lights flashing, siren wailing. She looked back at the nerds.

"Find him!" Was all she said, before storming off.

It was a twenty-minute walk to the Psi Cappa Alpha *Nerd's* dorm. Something bothered Cortney about Karen. Something about those eyes staring back at her in class the other night. *Maybe she is a vampire.* A few steps later, Cortney decided: *That's absurd, Cortney. Get a hold of yourself.*

Pedestrian traffic swarmed brisk and jovial on the sprawling campus. A new winter semester promised hope for students that survived the fall. She spotted Stocker near the far end of the campus. He walked straight toward her. Surely, he was bringing news about his cousin, Brice. He was coming from the direction of the nerd's frat house. The look on his face told her it would be *bad* news.

"Oh God. Please tell me he's ok."

"Nobody's seen him, Cortney. Not since your friend saw him with Karen. I got a bad feeling."

Cortney whipped out her cellphone and dialed 911.

"911 operator," a cheerful voice answered. *"Do you have an emergency?"*

"Yes," Cortney told her. "I want to report a missing person."

"A missing person?"

Cortney paced.

"That's right. He's been missing since Monday."

"Missing for how long?"

Is she gonna repeat everything I say?

"Since Monday."

"And what is your name, ma'am?"

"My name is Cortney Landau."

"Spell that, please?"

Stocker threw up his hands as Cortney spelled her name.

"And where are you located?"

"UCLA campus."

"You're on the campus?"

Cortney threw up a hand and shook her head.

"Yes."

"Ok, ma'am. I'm connecting you to UCLA campus police."

"No! Don't do that."

"Why not, ma'am?"

Cortney was incredulous.

"Because a crime has been committed. I need *real* police."

"I need you to calm down, ma'am."

"Calm *down*? I'm trying to report a possible kidnapping – or worse."

"I understand, ma'am. If there's been a crime committed on a college campus, we need to report it to the campus police, so that..."

"Oh, never mind. I can go there myself."

Cortney ended the call.

"What'd they say?" Stocker asked.

"They were gonna connect me to the campus police. Come on – I know the way."

Crowds thinned as noon classes started. The 911 operator called back as they walked.

"Ma'am, do you still want to report a crime?"

"We're walking to the campus police right now. So, never mind."

*****

When they got there Stocker did the talking. Officer Joe Roberts leaned across a messy desk as Stocker tried to convince him that a crime had been committed. This was a busy college campus where people cut class and went on trysts all the time. He was planning one himself. If the kid would only finish, so he could politely dismiss the matter and be on his way.

It wasn't until the mention of *Karen Okawa* that he fully engaged.

"So, wait. Slow down. I know that girl. She was just in here yesterday evening."

"What?" The accusers asked in unison.

"Just after sunset. She reported her boyfriend, Brice Maxwell, missing."

"What?"

"Stop it with the stereo," Joe told them while he eyed the two suspiciously. "And you come in here a day later lookin for the same Brice Maxwell?"

Stocker threw up his hands.

"You can't be serious?"

The woman, who hadn't yet identified herself, put her hands on his desk.

"That girl is dangerous. We've heard stories..."

"Young lady, first of all take your hands off my desk."

Joe stood up, to make sure she did.

"Karen told me that a woman from her class was yelling at him on Monday night."

"Yelling? Selena wasn't yelling at him. She was warning him. That girl is..."

Joe cut her off.

"Then your name would be Cortney Landau. Karen said it was _you_ that yelled at her."

"Well it wasn't. But what difference does it…"

Jealous lover. No wedding ring. "Miss Landau, just what is your relationship to Brice Maxwell?"

Now, the man seemed jealous of the woman.

"Brice Maxwell is my cousin."

Joe got closer to sniff the air for alcohol.

"So, what; this is some kind of lovers' quarrel?"

"Officer Maxwell…"

Don't try to con me, boy.

"Cortney called me as soon as Selena told her she saw them together. We've been trying to get in touch with him ever since."

So much for lunch with nurse Brenda. "Hold on a minute."

Joe pulled up his cell phone call log. 'Brenda Nurse' was the second name from the top.

"Hello."

"Hey Brenda. Yeah, I'm not gonna be able to meet you for lunch."

"Ok, Joe. But I'm not gonna be sittin' around waiting for you to get serious."

Joe tried not to frown, but by the looks on the kids' faces he knew he'd have to try harder.

"I know, I know. But something just came up."

"Hold on, Joe… Gotta go. There's a code blue in the emergency room."

Brenda had already hung up, when Joe said.

"Ok call you later. Bye,"

This better be important. "Pull up a chair, you two. Have a seat."

CHAPTER 21

South Eastern Belarus (Plus fourteen-hour time difference)

A svelte brunette sat pensive in her sumptuous quarters. When her call connected, she stood – like a tower.

"You idiot!"

"I'm not in the mood for chastisement, Nadia. What is it this time?"

"How dare you speak to me like that, you half-breed witch. Your victim is still alive. CNN is having a field day with the boy who lived after having his throat ripped out by a mountain lion."

"Don't worry. I covered my tracks. At worst, he'll turn. And never speak another human word."

"You've always been sloppy. If you mess this up, the Old Man won't have to kill you. I'll do it myself."

I loathe incompetence. Do I have to be everywhere at the same time? Now go and explain, before he sees it on the news.

Nadia was happy with what she saw in the mirror – after layers of make-up. Her riding boots stood on the other side of a coarse-haired bare skin rug. She strode across it missing the thing she treasured most – tactile sensation. She hated the Old Man from taking it from her. The life-size likeness of the former Nadia Roman hung, in oil on canvas, beside a long dead fireplace. Water wept from porous stone around the paint. And she stared at both while she tugged on well-worn, knee-high, leather boots.

Her door swung heavy on creaking hinges when she pulled it open. And she yelled at the first person she saw.

"Oil my hinges!"

Heavy footsteps echoed in the Great Hall as she marched past priceless antique statutes and paintings of Kathrine and Peter, the Greats. Ornate Greek fresco's, stolen in antiquity, hung at the far end of the hall where it narrowed and dead ended with a door on each side. On the left was the cast iron door that led to a bunker complex, two levels below. On the right was the Old Man's door; always open, so he could watch the bunker door.

"Come in, Nadia."

Vladimir sat watching CNN on his computer screen. His dwelling was simple; almost a cave. Dank, dark, and decrepit. And that incessant dripping of water pooled in puddles on his floor.

They spoke to each other in Russian. His attitude surprised her.

"Cannot be angry with Karen. It is our nature."

"She has no discipline. You should've sent me."

"If I could only laugh. Look at you. Taller than men. Older than men. And insistent on wearing my old boots. The only place *you* fit in is *here*."

"Why worry over boots when you never leave this room?"

The Old Man's back and neck cracked when he turned in his chair.

"I need fresh mud," he reminded her.

"I'll see to it."

"You said that yesterday."

Nadia sat in one of his simple wooden chairs and crossed her feet on a nearby table.

"Aren't you tired of this…this layer, where you live like some caveman? Don't you want the sun?"

"Patience my love."

"Don't call me that. You know I hate you."

"You didn't hate me when you married me."

"That was seventy years ago."

"Will you love me if I give you back the sun?"

If Nadia smiled, her face would crack new wrinkles.

"Will you give me back sensation? Will you give me a beating heart? Will you make me human again? I don't even have tears to cry, you bastard."

"There, there, poor Nadia," he said, wagging a boney finger at a table beside her. "A bowl of radio-active mud will warm your insides."

And then he gulped fresh blood from a silver chalice and passed it to her.

And she drank of it, and ate mud while he prattled on.

"What would you go back to, dear Nadia. Being a peasant among aristocrats? You would be long dead by now. Or would you go and wallow in the mud at Tunguska. Who saved you? I did. Vladimir Roman. And with Gregor to help us, we will take back the sun."

*****

Cortney drummed a pencil on Joe Robert's desk as he filled out the police report. Joe looked up – again.

"I asked you not to do that."

"Respectfully, officer Roberts – how much longer?"

"Just a couple more questions, miss Landau."

Both their cell phones vibrated at the same time. Cortney answered hers and walked to the far corner of the room.

"Hello?"

"Thank God."

"Dad?"

"It's all over the news. Are you all right?"

"What's all over the news?"

"That boy, attacked by a mountain lion on your campus."

Cortney locked eyes with Officer Roberts. And she knew – that he was hearing the same news. *Oh God – not Brice.*

"I gotta go, dad."

"Wait. Are you…"

Joe was finishing his conversation just as Cortney hung up.

"Thanks Brenda. I'll be right over."

Stocker was about to ask:

"Is it…"

Joe answered before he could finish.

"Yeah, it's Brice. Come on. You two can ride with me."

CHAPTER 22

Washington DC, UCLA, Southeastern Belarus
Wednesday, 19 January 2000 - 6pm Eastern Standard time

Gary and Jeff sat waiting in library reading room twenty-four.

"That *is* pretty bizarre, Gary. A mountain lion attack, on a college campus. I'm glad Cortney's safe."

"How do I *know* she's safe? She hung up on me – again."

A shadow moved outside the opaque, glass door. A tap on the glass announced Anne Li's entrance.

"Here you go, boys. Dig in."

She tossed a folder full of velums on the table, and they slid across it.

"Did you see anything, Anne," Jeff asked her.

"Hot off the press. I haven't looked."

Each of the three grabbed a stack of transparencies and held them, one by one, to the light. Gary squinted.

"What are we looking at, Anne?"

"Most recent pass of the DS-22 Polar Orbiting Recon Satellite. Right over the Chernobyl keep-out zone."

Gary shook his head.

"Then there's nothing here."

Jeff was quietly analyzing slides while they went back and forth.

"How do you know that without looking?" Karen asked.

Jeff chuckled, but without comment.

"One of the payloads on DS-22 is a Beta Particle Detector. If Beta particles were detected, these slides would be top secret."

"Come on, Gary. Beta particles can be blocked by a few inches of lead."

"More like five inches."

Jeff wheeled an overhead projector from the corner of the room, plugged it in, and turned it on.

"Anne, you outta know better than to argue with a Russian weapons expert by now. Let's have a closer look."

He centered a slide and focused the projection on the wall screen.

"Those hangers could hide SS-25 missile launchers. But no way those corrugated roofs could support five inches of lead."

The team looked at each of fifty-three slides.

"That's the last one," Anne announced.

Gary twisted his mouth in thought. Jeff spoke up.

"They could be hiding them underground."

Gary nodded in agreement.

"They *have* to be hiding them underground. Deep underground."

Anne agreed too.

"You're right. But how do we find them?"

*****

Nurse Brenda Daniels was standing in the Emergency Room parking lot when Officer Roberts skidded his cruiser to a stop. Stocker opened the rear door for Cortney. The UCLA Memorial Hospital rose in two wings above them. A news van was parked nearby with an antenna hoisted.

"This way," Brenda beckoned, in blue scrubs.

A group of police and fire emergency response crews stood in a circle, under the overhang outside the E.R. Roberts questioned *them* while Stocker and Cortney questioned the nurse.

"Brice Maxwell is my cousin."

Cortney assumed that only relatives would be allowed inside.

"And I'm his sister," she lied. "Can we see him?"

"I'm sorry," Brenda told them. "He was pronounced dead fifteen minutes ago."

"Oh God, no. I'm not really his sister. I shouldn't've lied."

"It's ok. I understand."

"How..." Stocker choked. "How did he die?"

"His carotid artery was punctured. He bled out."

A reporter and her cameraman wrapped up their broadcast.

"Aaaand – cut," the perky reporter in an overcoat told him.
Then her demeanor changed.

"Channel four is on their way to the crime scene. Let's get over there."
Her cameraman unshouldered his camera and *she* wrapped up cords.

"Nobody's ever seen a mountain lion on Wilshire Boulevard," the
cameraman grumbled. "What a bunch a bull."
Brenda must've overheard him and snapped:

"You didn't see his throat."

"Has anyone called his mom?" Stocker asked of no one in particular.
A fireman answered.

"She's on the way."

Cortney's back was to the emergency room doors when the commotion
broke through.

"Oh shit! Frank, get that camera back up."
Cortney was almost afraid to look. But when she did her senses were
assaulted by a blood-soaked monster. Its voice was deep and garbled. It
smelled like a days-dead animal.

"Ahhhh!" Brice wailed. "Let me go! You're hurting me!"

A gaunt, gray Brice Maxwell raged against the laws of nature, and those that
would rather he behave more like a dead man.

"Get him!" A doctor yelled, as Brice dragged three men.

"God, look at him! Hurry up, Frank. In three, two, one. This is Carmen
Murphy - Channel two news with a follow-up, on…"

Brice charged right over the cameraman, knocking him to the polished
concrete.

"Stocker, help meee," Brice cried with words spoken in slow motion.
He seemed oblivious to the wreckage of medical equipment dragged along
by tubes and wires.

"Somebody stop him!" A doctor covered in blood pleaded.

Brice's clothes hung off him, where they had been cut away by the medical
team, revealing dried blood, fresh blood and the blotchy skin of a battered
corpse. Cortney backed away as Brice reached to embrace his cousin.

"I'm not dead," he gurgled. "Tell them I'm not dead."

Emergency response teams charged him. But he tossed them aside like rag
dolls.

"Calm down, man," Stocker pleaded with outstretched hands. "You
gotta let them help you."

Brice collapsed on Stocker with a loving embrace, saying:

"I love you, man," before sinking his teeth into his cousin's neck.

Cortney heard a woman's blood curdling scream...for seconds...before realizing it was her own.

Gun shots rang out. Brice stepped back and checked his side for holes. There were many. Thick, tarry colored blood oozed from his wounds. Pathetic, unblinking, eyes stared out from his sunken gray face; as if he were trying to figure out why he was being shot.

"Please," he said, and turned back to Stocker's bleeding throat. "I need it. Just let me have it."

And he staggered, like a wounded wolf, back to its prey.

Bullets peppered his blotchy face. Pink smoked exploded in wisps from the other side of his head. He fell like an axed tree and twitched on the floor...for the next ten minutes.

*****

"Nadia?"

"What! Can't you see we are talking?"

"Sorry, mistress. But the *Valley People* are at the gates again?"

"And what are they doing?"

"Begging for food, and..."

"And what, you oaf?"

"It is dawn. They need...I mean they *want* shelter from the sun."

Nadia jumped to her feet, distaining the mud on her favorite boots.

"Useless vermin. Let them starve. Let them burn!"

Vladimir intervened.

"Sit down, Nadia! Have you no compassion?"

A defiant Nadia stood.

"And what do you know about compassion? You *did* this to me."

"Sit, and I will tell you."

She sat.

"Boy," Vladimir addressed the cowering servant. "Let them in outer sanctum. And give them one live goat.

Nadia seethed while her master – her husband – her maker, explained himself.

"For decades you go back and forth, to make a life outside. Those at gates are of your making. But you always come back. In here..." he spread out his arms. "...where you are Queen. Out there you are no better than

Valmpir at gates.

I was not always callous mercenary you met in youth. I was once loving family man. I was soldier, loyal to family dynasty. My cousin was Czar, devoted to family and country. He was undone by misguided wife. Him, wife, and four children – were spirited away in night, by opposition.

Scheduled for execution, they were. Vladimir, sneak onto the death squad – pretending to kill – hoping to save – shooting in air."

Vladimir's head hung low. Long tangled hair covered his grotesque face.

"Vladimir could only save one girl, *Anna*, by pretending to finish her off. There was…so much gore that dead were not easy to count. Vladimir brought her here. He hid her here for ten years."

Vladimir moaned, tearless.

"For this good deed, they killed my wife and son. After that, Vladimir change his sir-name, to hide. He had no heart. He killed – first the opposition – then for money…then for sport. He was bitten by Tunguska Valley People, on silly trip for rocks. The skinny girl called them Valmpir. I came home looking for Anna. By then Vladimir a bloodthirsty Valmpir. Could not find her.

CHAPTER 23

Cortney followed the gurney, as they wheeled Stocker through the double doors of the E.R. The bloody doctor stopped them just inside.

"No! He can't come back in here. Put him in isolation. STAT!"
Cortney turned around to find herself on the business side of freshly laid police tape.

"Listen up everybody. I'm doctor Tobias Hardyway; Chief Surgeon on Call. And I'm declaring this area a level one CDC emergency. Get it cordoned off."

Cortney creeped toward the tape line while he went on.

"I want every square inch of this blood covered with powered lye."

"What about the body?" Someone asked.

"The body too. If you have one drop of blood on you, you'll need to be screened. Stand over there."

Tobias eyed Cortney up and down as she stepped backward over the crime tape. She looked herself over as he inspected her. No blood. No bloody footprints.

"You can go," he finally told her.

He looked at the cameraman who'd fallen. He was covered with blood.

"You. Over there!"
Carmen, the newscaster rubbed up against Frank.

"Are you kidding me?" Tobias admonished her. "You too. Over there."
Doctor Hardyway stuck out his chin towards a young doctor outside the police tape.

"Jason! Call the CDC. Tell them what happened here."

Then he looked at the crowd of seven that were tainted by blood.

"All of you. Follow me."

*****

At quarter past eleven, Gary and Jeff were still in the bowels of the Library's sub-floors, with a pile of Belarussian newspapers stacked at their feet. Jeff unfolded another one and yawned.

"You know, Gary; I can't read Russian, but I keep seeing pictures that remind me of Cortney's mountain lion. What does this one say?"

Gary took the paper and opened it to a story buried in back of the tabloid. A picture of a corpse with its throat ripped open was under the caption.

"Third Mutilation This Year."

Gary continued translating for Jeff.

"Animal attacks are on the increase. Be careful not to stray off alone. Especially at night. The latest victim only went out to bring his mail inside. He was found gored in his throat by the post stop."

Gary looked up.

"How many?"

"Six in the last four months," Jeff picked up another paper from the stack he'd gone through. He thumbed to a back page. "And look at this." Gary translated the caption above a fuzzy black and white picture of a sinister face.

"Beware The Valmpir Bloodsuckers."

The librarians locked eyes. Jeff must've read Gary's mind.

"No reception down here."

"Yeah – I gotta go up top and call Cortney."

Gary was almost out the door, when:

"Hold on a minute, Gary."

Gary turned around.

"Here she is. Her name is Nadia Roman."

"Yep, that's her. See what you can find out while I'm upstairs."

*****

Cortney sat in her usual seat that night. She made it a point not to look back at Karen. With her phone in her lap, on silent, she texted.

'Hurry. Class almost over.'

Done, a text came back.

She was surprised when her phone lit up with an incoming call. *Not now, Dad.* Her concern was apparently evident on her face.

"Miss Landau," Professor Richter blasted her. "I've indulged your cellphone antics all night. Give it to me."

A wide-eyed Cortney shook her head to the negative.

"Would you rather I failed you?"

Cortney reluctantly gave him the phone. On no. *He's not actually gonna read it.*

But he did.

"Let's see here…Hurry. Class almost over. A hot date, have we miss Landau?"

The classes laughter obscured his next sentence.

"And Gizmo answered back, 'Done.' You can pick this up after class. Next time turn it off. There will be no texting in this class…"

Cortney turned, ever so slowly, to see if Karen might have been tipped off by the not so cryptic message. Karen glared back at her…not batting an eye.

*****

Nadia glared, not batting an eye, when Gregor entered her ready room.

"What part of one pm did you not understand, Gregor?"

Dozens of humans and once-humans sat in metal chairs, in a large masonry room with fluorescent lighting. The non-humans sipped oxygenated blood from thermos-like contraptions. The humans wore dill green radiation suits. Eight key team members sat around a rectangular, wooden table. Once human, Gregor, took his place among them. Stacks of currency; Euro's and American dollars formed a center piece on the table.

"Why are we here?" Queen Nadia asked her faithful following.

"To change the world." Most answered in unison.

"Why are we here?" She yelled louder.

"To change the world!"

Nadia pranced tall and proud in her camouflaged fatigues. A ponytail protruded from the hole in the back of her fatigue cap. A vailed Vladimir sat quietly, alone.

"That is our aim. To change the world. By destroying the West. We do it for freedom. And for the pleasure of walking in the light of the sun. We are a new breed, poised on the brink of history, to take over the…"

Doctor Helena Heinrich, who sat at the table, dared to interrupt.

"Forgive me mistress but, technically, you are not a breed because you cannot reproduce. So, you must be careful to live in symbiosis with your…"

"I do not need to be reminded of that which I miss most, Helena!" Nadia raged. "Now you have a choice to make. Join our kind, or die in agony from radiation poisoning."

"I meant no harm," Helena pleaded. "I only meant to point out the precarious nature of your being. If you kill too many, you will starve. If you create too many, you will starve."

Helena trembled. Her whole suit shook as Nadia approached her from behind. Nadia snatched off the woman's hood and ripped open her radiation suit.

"Now choose!"

"No. Please?"

The woman broke for the door. Nadia leapt over her and punched her in the face. Her nose gushed blood and fell over on the floor. The once-humans all lusted her blood.

"Nyet!" Nadia bellowed. "She is mine alone. Now Doctor Merchant, would you please explain our biology to the uninformed? Can you do so without insult?'

A once-human Englishman stood and inhaled deeply.

"I'd say that I look and behave rather normal. Wouldn't you agree?" Dill green radiation hoods with clear beryllium faceplates nodded vigorously.

"It is because I breathe. Even though we don't have to – we breath. Our circulatory systems are not like yours. Our hearts do not beat. Our parasitic super-friends have altered us. They have made us supermen, by boring holes between the chambers of our hearts. They swim through us, carrying super oxygenated blood through our bodies. And thus, we crave the oxygenated blood flowing through your arteries."

He pointed at the woman bleeding on the floor. Many of Nadia's kind could barely restrain themselves. Nadia wagged a gloved finger at them.

"I'll kill the first one of you that defies my rule."

Doctor Merchant went on.

"It is by breathing that we have kept our humanity. Vladimir was the first to discover that we could keep our lungs alive. Those outside belch, to force air over their vocal cords. They can only grunt. By breathing we speak and socialize. By breathing we can suck blood from a small incision, rather than rip the host apart like an animal. But it was Gregor who discovered that radiation preserves our human appearance."

Those without heartbeats cheered and raised their gruesome flasks.

"Were it not for Gregor, we would look like walking corpses. It was he, being a nuclear physicist, who melted down the reactor at Chernobyl."

Gregor stood and took a bow to the applause of everyone not wearing a radiation suit.

"And now, Generalissimo Ivan Petrov; tell us how you will alter the planet to suit our biology."

The pickle-suited general stood in his place.

"We will darken the sun and irradiate the West, to embolden a new regime. A small price to pay to for the resurgence of the Soviet Union. Screen!"

A wall screen flickered to life and played a video simulation of a preemptive nuclear strike. Twenty-two SS-25B mobile launchers rolled out of the weapons cavern and lined up along a winding road. They launched computer animated missiles, one by one.

A widescreen shot of a pseudo earth showed warheads striking a corridor across the United States. A brown dust cloud formed around the fortieth parallel. A ground shot of the sun, reddened by airborne dust shinned on the ruins. And Nadia's kind walked in its light.

"Thank you, Generalissimo," Nadia clapped. "We salute you. Finance!"

A radiation suited, middle-aged woman shared from her chair.

"To my fellow pickle-heads," she said, referring to the humans. "We couldn't care less about the color of the sun at the fortieth parallel. Our care is sitting here on this table."

The human claps were muffled by gloves. But they clapped.

"Eight million, in Euros. Six million in American dollars. Drug money brought in by our drug kingpin, Mani Juarez, in a single week. You human operatives will get your cut at the end of the meeting."

A chant broke out.

"Go Mani, go Mani, go Mani…"

To which the five-foot-six pudgy human stood and danced.

Stella, the asset manager took back the floor. We have one-point two trillion dollars in our collective coffers; mainly from seventy years of compound interest on our founder's initial investments.

"A hand for our leader."

She bowed to Vladimir, to raucous applause. Vladimir gave a slight bow from his seat.

"Now spend those dollars. They'll be worthless in a week."

"Thank you, Stella," Nadia gave a curt clap. "We have a few problems." The room quieted.

"One of our American infiltrators has been careless. At this very moment, American doctors are examining the blood of her victim. They cannot be allowed to discover our nature prematurely. The Sweeper is on his way to California to clean up the mess. From here on, if you err you will die. NO MORE MISTAKES!

And now for those subhuman maggots parading the perimeter by night. They are not to be fed. And I want new razor wire on the fences. Is that clear?"

"Yes Mistress," someone yelled from the back of the room.

"I am sick to death of this infernal drip, drip, drip. Everywhere I go, the walls drip. The ceiling drips."

"Mistress, one of the pumps has failed," an unsuited man pointed out.

"WELL THEN FIX IT! Pay those people, and get them out of here."

While money was passed out, Nadia dragged her victim from the room. A trail of blood led to her quarters, where Nadia took to her pleasure.

CHAPTER 24

Karen made sure she left Professor Richter's class after Cortney Landau got her phone back. She heard Cortney shush him when he tried to talk about it.

"Miss Landau. I'm not at all comfortable with your attitude."

Karen saw Cortney glance at her during the exchange.

"I'm sorry, Professor Richter, but I really have to go."

Karen followed her at a distance. Two of Brice's other friends met Cortney in the hallway. They all stared at Karen and rushed outside the building.

Karen followed them at a distance. *What are you bags of blood up to?* Each time they looked back at her, she was more certain that: *They know I did it. I know that they know. And they know that I know. What a mess. I could kill all three of them, right now, and hide the bodies.*

And she pictured killing them. Then she pictured Nadia beheading her with one of the sharp-edged weapons in her torture chamber. She rubbed her throat and decided that her prey could wait until the bombs fell.

*****

Cortney tried in vain not to look back at Brice's killer.

"She knows."

Trevor glanced back.

"How do you know she knows? Maybe she just doesn't like you."

"I'm telling you, she knows."

"How could she know? She was in class with you. Just keep walking."

*****

Karen looked around for prying eyes before she unlocked her front door. Inside, she checked every window, making sure they were still locked. Then she went to check her stash. *Somethings wrong.* In the kitchen, in front of the refridgerator, under the door...lie sticky wheel marks on the floor.

Dammit! I thought I cleaned that up. She opened the refridgerator door. Everything was as it should be. Human food: ketchup, milk carton, cheese, beer, etc; all exactly where she'd placed it two months earlier. And not a trace of blood – except on the floor. She looked down again.

"Dammit, Karen! Pay attention."

*****

Cortney, Trevor, and Gizmo sat in the boys' dorm room, staring at a squiggly line on the screen of Gizmo's desktop computer.

"It's working," Gizmo beamed, and turned up the volume.
"Who's she talking to?" Trevor asked.
"Shhhh," Gizmo shushed him. "She's talking to herself. Quiet."

Cortney's phone vibrated in her pocket. The boys looked at her. She checked the caller I.D.

"It's my dad."
She remembered he'd called earlier.
"He's worried about me. I better answer it."
"Quiet!" Gizmo ordered. "Call him back later. What's that noise?"
"Uh oh," Trevor answered.
Gizmo looked up from the line that jiggled with each sound that Karen made.

"Uh oh, what?"
"She's pulling out the refrigerator."
"Why would she be pulling out the refrigerator?"

Cortney's stomach dropped.
"How do you know what her refrigerator sounds like being pulled out?"
The squiggly line filled the full screen when Karen screamed.
"Mother----ers!"
Trevor reached in his pocket while she cursed.

*****

"Where is it?"

Karen turned over the refrigerator with the stroke of her hand.

*****

Gizmo turned down the volume at the sound of a crash. Cortney associated the sound of Karen's tantrum with the stupid look on Trevor's beet-red face.

"What did you do, Trevor?"

Trevor held up a little metal box, about the size of a can of sardines.

"Come on, man," Gizmo admonished. "I told you not to touch anything."

"What is that?" Cortney asked with a tapping foot.

Karen was still raging when Trevor answered.

"I don't know. I can't get it open."

Gizmo snatched the box from Trevor.

"Give it here."

He examined it with his eyes, then tested it with his fingers and thumbs.

"It's a puzzle box."

"A what?" Cortney asked.

Gizmo paused, before giving Cortney a thoughtful look.

"Like super, child-proofed. You can't open it unless you know where to push."

Cortney nodded.

"How'd you know it was there, Trevor?'

"I saw wheel marks on the kitchen floor…"

Karen wailed, *"I'll kill you all,"* just as Trevor added. "…in blood."

CHAPTER 25

Nurse Brenda stood quietly, at the nurses' station, awaiting an opportunity to protest her isolation. But the phone rang again as soon as Doctor Hardyway hung up.

"Hold on, Brenda. Hardyway here."

Brenda, hearing the man reading Doctor Hardyway the riot act, waited for the fireworks. Tobias was generally impatient with his superiors, as well as his subordinates. It didn't take long before he blew up.

"Now you wait just a damn minute, Bob. Technically, that boy was already dead when they wheeled him into the E.R... That's right; I said already dead...We didn't call it because he was still conscious."

More yelling from the other end. *I'm not gonna get out of here anytime soon. I better call my sister to pick up the kids – once Toby gets Bob Anderson straightened out.*

"His heart wasn't beating, Bob. The paramedics couldn't find a pulse because he didn't have one. He wasn't breathing either."

A light on another button indicated an incoming call.

"Hold one, Bob...Hardyway...Leave it in the airlock tray."

Tobias lifted his chin to Brenda. *He could've at least called me by name.*

The doctor's voice trailed off as Brenda walked to the airlock door at the near end of the corridor. She pushed the lighted green button for access, and waited for the lock to click. Ionized air was still hissing in the specimen tray, before the ionized air shower came on. Dutifully, she raised her arms in a slow pirouette while ionized air refreshed her, shift old, underarms.

The dead man's toxicology report was in the specimen tray, between thick plastic doors. She wished she could just keep on walking through the outer airlock door and go home.

*****

"Sorry, Jeff," Gary apologized for being gone so long. "She's not answering."

He'd tried calling Cortney three times over a half an hour.

"What'd you find out?"

"Nadia Roman. Age seventy. Worked for the Belarussian Ministry of the Interior from…October ninety-eight to March ninety-nine."

Gary thought he'd misunderstood Jeff, or that Jeff had misspoken.

"Did you say she was seventy?"

"Yep. I checked three different sources. I'm thinkin she doesn't look a day over forty. The magic of makeup, I guess. Anyway, she was a dedicated employee. First to work – last to leave,"

Gears turned in Gary's head.

"That would leave plenty of time for her to meddle. Where is she now?"

"Not a trace of her anywhere," Jeff told him.

"Ok, let's work backward."

*****

The amplitude modulated line on Gizmo's screen came alive with Karen's rant.

"She's on the phone," Gizmo reported.

"*Nyet, Nadia…Nyet, Nadia…Nyet, Nyet, Nyet!*"

Karen went on, but the conversation was mostly unintelligible. Cortney understood very little of the Russian being spoken.

"Ok, that's Russian," Cortney said with certainty "She's talking to someone named Nadia. Something about going…no…leaving. I don't understand most of it, but Nadia wants her to stay."

Gizmo's eyes narrowed.

"Where'd you learn Russian?"

"I only know a little. My dad speaks fluent Russian – from his old job."

"Was he a spy or something?" Trevor asked.

To her own surprise, Cortney had to answer:

"Maybe. But we should be recording this."

Gizmo was way ahead of her.

"We've got the whole thing. You can play it for your dad when she hangs up."

Cortney tried to do just that.

"No answer, guys. Can we send him an audio file?"

Gizmo stuck a thumb in the air.

"Dad," Cortney began after the beep. "I'm sending you an audio file. It's a phone call – in Russian. My friends and I think the women on the phone killed our friend, Brice – the boy on the news. Call me when you get it."

Then she looked at the boys.

"It's almost midnight in D.C. He's probably asleep."

And once she thought of the implications of Karen's not so vailed threat, she asked:

"Can I crash here tonight?"

*****

Gary and Jeff sat, logged in, at adjacent computer stations on subfloor four.

"Look at this, Jeff."

Gary showed Jeff a mottled image of a Belarusian certificate of marriage.

"Nadia Kensky married a man named Vladimir Roman in nineteen-forty-five when she was twenty-five years old."

Gary relinquished his seat to Jeff.

"You stay on her," Jeff said as he moved to the next empty station. "I'll see what I can dig up on *him*."

*****

Nadia was prepared to burst, as usual, through Vladimir's open door. But it was closed. The sound of her stone hand pounding on thick wood reverberated through the empty main hall. Her subjects always hid when they saw her coming.

"Vladimir!"

Vladimir opened the door, not wearing his veil.

"What is it now, my precious?"

"Don't patronize me, you old dog. Karen has been compromised."

"Meaning what?"

"Someone broke in and stole her Cobalt pellets"

"Could it be she has misplaced them?"

"They were STOLEN! She must be eliminated before she is questioned."

Nadia thought Vladimir looked like a mummy without the veil. He shook his morbid head.

"Karen will not break."

"She will. Already, she craves Cobalt. She'll go mad in two days. The sweeper is in America. She must be erased, along with her mistakes."

Vladimir hesitated for a moment.

"Have your way with her. Leave no loose ends."

*****

Jeff sat at the station that Gary first logged into.

"Hey, Gary; who'd be emailing you, at this time of night?"

"Who's it from?"

"TheGiz."

CHAPTER 26

Washington D.C.
Thursday, 19 January

Gary boarded a coach seat on the first morning flight bound for Los Angeles International Airport. There was a problem in the first-class cabin. A rotund man blocked the aisle as he struggled to force his over-stuffed carry-on into the overhead bin. A tall blonde man forced his way past, knocking the man into the wide first-class seat in front of him. The man's roller bag fell from the compartment onto the small of his back.

The hero in Gary spoke up for the downed passenger.

"Hey buddy!" Gary began, but was cut off by another man closer to the culprit.

"You don't have to be an asshole! This guy paid for a seat, just like you did!"

The blonde man's stare was like ice. The Good Samaritan choked to silence. Gary knew the look. If you had plans for the day, you didn't want mess with *this* guy. Gary was bound to protect his daughter from the jaws of a global death plot. *Let it go, Gary.*

*****

Tobias, weary from sleepless hours, watched on closed circuit TV as Doctor Corine Rodriguez, fully suited in environmental protection garb, began the autopsy on Brice.

"The subject is a nineteen year old male. His body is covered with third and fourth degree, post mortem burns, from powdered lye disinfectant."

She began the internal exam with a Y incision, beginning from each shoulder just below the clavicle, meeting at the upper sternum and continuing to the top of the pelvis.

She had to lean on the scalpel to cut through the dermal tissues, and then she needed help getting through the musculature because it was so hard. When she folded back the skin and muscle tissue. it creaked like wood. Her assistant, Doctor Forester, used a vibrating saw to cut through the ribs on each side of the sternum. The team gasped in unison when she lifted the breastplate clear of the chest. Doctor Hardyway pressed his intercom button.
"Zoom in on the heart."

The heart was shriveled. The lungs were days dead and had dried to the consistency of jerky. They were shriveled to a forth of their normal size. Debate broke out in the observation room when Tobias asked the quarantine team:
"How was he mobile, semi-functional, and as strong as a horse just twenty-four hours ago?"

The condition of the thoracic organs momentarily diverted their attention. The digestive tract was a stark contrast to the heart and lungs. The stomach was several times the size of a normal specimen. Doctor Rodrigues probed it.
"The stomach muscle is rigid – like an inflated tire," she reported. "The liver, gallbladder, and pancreas are pushed into abnormal positions by the enlarged stomach."
Protruding blood vessels swarmed over the stomach like garter snakes.
"Gastral vascular vessels are swollen and distended."

Doctor Hardyway interrupted.
"Zoom in on the liver, please."

The cecal trunk and gastrointestinal arteries all dwarfed the thoracic aorta, normally the largest artery in the body. The liver was grossly enlarged, as was the portal vein that transports blood from the digestive tract to the liver.
"The digestive system has obviously taken on some elevated level of importance," Tobias observed aloud. "The deceased's portal vein is as thick as my arm . . ."

Brice's dead body gave three quick twitches.

"The deceased...," Doctor Forester interrupted, "is still moving."

"We've been over this a half-dozen times!" Carmen said. "He's dead. His heart stopped beating days ago, and his breathing shortly after that. He has no f---ing brain!" She looked up at the camera, and then quietly added: "Tighten his restraints."

"Proceed, please," Tobias advised.

Doctor Forester switched on the suction motor and held an embalmer's trocar ready to consume the contents of Brice's stomach. As Corine began an incision into the stomach, he said:

"We'll need more bags. His stomach must contain a gallon of...."

He was cut off as the stomach erupted with such force that it propelled Corine's scalpel across the room. And it spewed a high-pressure jet of blood into the ceiling tiles for almost a full minute before it subsided. The autopsy team jumped back. Blood pooled on the floor until it covered the soles of their contamination proof boots.

CHAPTER 27

Jeff had only gotten a few hour of sleep after he and Gary left the library. He half nodded as Judy Haynsworth called the morning meeting to order.

"I just left a secret briefing at the Whitehouse," she began. "General Beauregard believes that the hijackers are using a large underground complex to hide the missing equipment. The Joint Chiefs are weighing options to ascertain the location, and..."

She's gonna take twenty minutes to parrot the briefing. How was she chosen over Gary? Judy droned on with buzz-words and paraphrases, most of which would be on CNN by noon.

Jeff cleared his throat.

"Excuse me, Judy," he didn't wait to be recognized. "Gary and I have actionable intelligence. We were all ready profiling three Belarussian operatives when..."

Judy didn't seem to care.

"Where's Gary?"

"He left for Los Angeles this morning to follow up on..."

"Los Angeles? On *whose* authority?"

Jeff tried not to raise his voice.

"We got a tip late last night. A recorded conversation, *in Russian*, between two..."

"I didn't authorize any recording. What recording?"

How could Jeff explain that three kids just happened to record someone very likely talking the very same Nadia that he and Gary were profiling?

"While we were profiling a woman with ties to Soviet physicist, Markov

Gregor…"

A man in a newish white button-down and the latest power tie interrupted.

"Markov Gregor died at Chernobyl."

"We thought so too, Mike. But we saw a picture of him with a woman named…"

Judy was tapping her foot.

"No crosstalk please. Get to the point, Jeff.'

"The woman's name is Nadia Roman. At one time, she was married to Vladimir Roman – AKA Vladimir Romanov, second cousin to Nickolas Romanov…"

"The point, Jeff?"

"We think we know where they're hiding the missiles."

Judy never liked Gary. Everybody knew it. She'd tried to one up him, every chance she got. Her eyes looked like a bloodthirsty wolf. *Oh, the irony.*

"Based on what?" She asked with hands on hips.

"We were looking at Belarussian news reports about a series of human mutilations. They bared a striking similarity to an alleged animal attack near the UCLA campus. Three students bugged the apartment of…"

"Ok, stop right there. A dead physicist…" she counted on her fingers. "…a dead Russian Czar, animal attacks, and three students bugging an apartment. Why does this sound like that cartoon show about the dog and the pesky kids?" She paused for effect. "What's it called?"

Several answered in unison:

"Scooby Doo."

*****

Gary's flight touched down at 8:15 am, Los Angeles time. He grabbed his laptop case from under the seat in front of him, and his gym bag from the overhead. Gary was out the aircraft door before the first-class passengers unbuckled their seat belts. He made straight for the car rental, calling Cortney along the way.

Gary was half way to UCLA before she finally answered.

"Hello?"

"Cortney it's Dad. Where are you?"

"Dad? I just woke up; why?"

"I got your email. Did you take something from Karen's apartment?"

"My friend did. Hold on, I'll get it."

"No! Don't go near it. Get as far away from it as you can."

"Why, Dad; what is it?"

"It's radioactive Cobalt. Oh, God – you didn't touch it, did you?"

"No, Dad. We couldn't get the puzzle box open."

Gary's heart pounded as he zig-zagged through rush hour traffic.

"Leave the box in your room and come down stairs. I'll be there in twenty minutes."

"What? Twenty minutes? Dad, where are you?"

"Northbound on the 405."

"What? You're here in LA?"

"Cortney, you have no idea what you've gotten yourself into. Get to a public place – right now."

"I'm not at home, Dad. I'm at my friends' place. It's on Fraternity Row."

Gary's fatherly side kicked in.

"You're with a boy?"

"No, Dad. It's not what you think."

"You're probably safer there, anyway. Give me the address – I'll meet you out front."

CHAPTER 28

Chaos ruled as noisy crowds grew outside the double doors of the UCLA Memorial Hospital emergency room. A cameraman dressed in winter's warmest shuddered in the frosty bite of January as he panned the crowd with a shoulder held camera.

Police sirens blared in the background as plumes of exhaled condensation rose above the raucous crowd. The camera man, Patrick Broom, had his mind half way around the world, where his camera feed was surely being scrutinized by rage filled eyes.

News crews worked with frenzied purpose as they raced to be first on air. All around him, the Russian cameraman kept hearing the same word, from some too old to be students.

"He was a vampire," a man told the wide eyed old woman beside him.

"There's no such thing as a vampire," from the man behind the first man.

"I hear they have another one inside!"

"Did he turn into a bat?" A young woman; probably a student, laughed.

And then there were the groupies, dressed in all black Gothic attire. Peter thought them silly. Half the crowd was excited, the other half scared; all jostling to see through the double doors. An overwhelmed hospital security guard gave way to the press of the crowd. Peter heard him call for backup on his walkie talkie.

"Joe, we're gonna need more backup."

One by one, news crews took to the air. The Russian pointed his camera at the brunette news caster, with perfectly applied make up and a bright orange coat as she faced her camera crew. A man rolled a boom microphone over her head and signaled with his fingers as he counted down:

"Three, two, one."

"This is Carmen Murphy – channel two news, with a follow-up on yesterday's carnage at UCLA Memorial Hospital. Believe it or not, all these people have been drawn here to see the man they say is a vampire…"

The Russian panned away toward police cars as they fishtailed into the hospital parking lot. He was startled by a female voice shouting in Russian.

"Peter! Did you bring more cobalt? Peter, please! I'm burning!"

How fortuitous. The hare has come to the fox. "Of course I did, Karen. But not here. I went to your apartment looking for you."

Karen shivered, *sweating*, under an umbrella. Clearly, the disfigurement was under way. Gray and blue patches of dead skin showed through poorly applied makeup.

"I went looking for my stolen pellets at the room of the American girl."

"Nadia told you to stay away from her."

"I couldn't hold out. I thought I might find her here. Please."

"She may still be in the company of the two boys."

Peter looked around for privacy.

"You can't be seen here. You're already starting to change."

Carmen stuck a hand mike into a man's face. "Can I ask you why you're out here in the cold?"

"How often do you hear of a vampire outside of Hollywood," the man said with a wink.

Carmen gave an obligatory smile and asked, "Do you actually believe he's a real vampire?"

"I don't know," the man laughed. "But this sure beats sitting at home watching it on the news."

A young woman in black pushed her way through the crowd.

"We believe."

She was flanked by a man and two women, all dressed in Gothic Black attire from head to toe. The girl brushed aside jet-black hair, revealing black lipstick and eye makeup.

"He *is* real. Us…" she motioned toward her cadre of misfits. "We're just lifestyle vampires. But I always believed,"

"Thank you," Carmen tried to dismiss the girl in black. "And what about you sir, why are…"

The girl in black beamed at the news woman and moved back in to the frame. "We've been waiting for him. He's our savior."

Carmen frowned.

"Your savior?"

"I have to get to him. I want to live forever…"

"Okay, cut!" The man with the boom mike yelled.

"No." Carmen shouted to her cameraman. "Keep rolling. Young lady," Carmen shook her head. "You're serious, aren't You?"

"Yes," the girl answered. "Totally serious. I'm ready to be changed."

A wall of police officers pushed back the crowd.

"Okay folks – please. You're blocking the hospital entrance. Move it along. That's right – keep moving."

Carmen shot a perfect smile at her camera.

"And there you have it folks; a vampire in Westwood. Back to you, Hal."

Peter heard the next words through his earpiece.

"I've seen enough. Find them first, then take care of Karen. Bomb the hospital as planned. Your weapons are under the spare tire. We will extract you at Van Nuys Airport."

*****

Gary hugged Cortney tight, and held on, while Gizmo ran to get the puzzle box. Pavilax looked down on his charge, knowing that this moment was the calm before a terrible storm.

That old serpent, the Devil; called Satan, and Beelzebub – Lord of the flies, was also Lord of the parasitic microbes. He'd marveled that his primordial spawn had survived, for ten thousand years, on an icy comet. Orbital mechanics overcame great odds to rain pieces of the comet down on the Tunguska River Valley.

Satan coaxed a family of hunters far past the edge of their territory to be present at the event. And he protected them from the blast. One of the siblings would vector the Oxygen Thieves into the human race. The Devil nursed his hosts, the Valley People, like infants until Sir Cedrick was compelled by demonic forces to seek cosmic treasure in the Valley. And now, Satan's plan to bring his oxygen thirsty bugs into the atomic age was made perfect, in Nadia's legions.

Presently, two of Satan's demonic lieutenants hovered above Peter and Karen. In demon-speak, they conversed.

"There he is. The girl's protector betrays her whereabouts."

"But Pavilax is a formidable foe. Surely we need greater numbers."

"Silence, you coward. We will be rewarded for defeating him. Let us lead our charges into battle."

*****

"I need you to focus, Karen," Peter told the faltering Valmpir. "Where are the two boys?"
Karen shook.
"Give me the pellets, Peter."
"After you lead me to the loose ends," he lied.
"I could kill you and take them."

Peter laughed, confident of his bluff. He hadn't come to dose Karen. He came to kill her.
"They are shielded in lead. You won't find them. Nor will you sense their presence. Find the boys and you will have two puzzle boxes."
"Alright," Karen snarled. "I was going there next, anyway."

Peter extended his hand.
"I have a car — a few blocks from here."
"It's not that far," Karen told him. "We can walk."
"Your pills are in the car," he lied again. *I'll need my weapons.*

CHAPTER 29

Gary inspected the puzzle box.

"It's made of Lead alloy," he said with certainty. "We'll be ok; it's shielded."

"What do we do next?" Cortney asked, zipping her coat.

"*We* find her. *I* question her. Come on. I have a car down the block."

An unusually strong, easterly gust, came out of nowhere as they crossed the intersection at the end of the block. Paper trash, and newspaper leavings took Gary's attention as they blew past. And there, halfway down the block to the east, Gary saw the blonde menace from the plane. *You!*

"Dad, that's her."

"Huh?"

"Karen – getting in the Black truck with that man."

He's the hitman. "It figures."

"What figures?"

"Never mind. Get out of sight."

Cortney back-peddled and ducked into the Westwood Bakery. Gary and the boys followed her lead. The black SUV containing a murderer, and a probable hitman cruised slowly by and made a right on Fraternity Row. Gizmo was first to guess.

"She's looking for us. I wonder who the guy is?"

"Trust me, son," Gary warned. "You don't wanna know."

"Why, Dad? Do you know him?"

"He's the man Nadia sent to clean up Karen's mess. She called him 'The Sweeper.' The three of you stay put. I'll take it from here."

Gary dashed for his car. Cortney ran behind him. He had no choice but to let her in, before she was spotted.

"Hurry. Get in and duck."

Gary started his compact as the killers' vehicle crept up the block.

"They don't know which house is theirs'," he told Cortney. "I'm gonna let you out around the block and cut them off at the next corner."

"I'd rather stay with you, Dad," Cortney cried. "I'm sorry I've been…"

Gary thought Cortney was about to apologize. But he didn't have time to indulge her.

"No, Cortney," he told her.

His left turn threw her against the passenger door.

"These people are dangerous."

"I know they are. She killed my friend. I don't want anything to happen to *you*."

Gary raced to the next parallel block and fishtailed a right.

"It's bigger than that, Cortney. If we don't stop them, *millions* will die."

He made an abrupt stop in the middle of the block.

"Cortney?"

She kissed Gary and turned to get out of the car. Gary felt it right to add:

"If I don't make it, call your Uncle Jeff, and tell him what happened here."

Cortney didn't answer. Nor did she look back. Gary would've loved to put her back in the car and take her someplace far away from this nightmare. But she wouldn't be safe anywhere if he didn't stop Nadia. He sped for the corner to cut off the SUV. *Karen will have to talk. I have her Cobalt. Somehow, it's keeping her alive.*

Gary made a right and sped toward the intersection. But Cortney's touching protest delayed him, just enough for the SUV to beat him to the intersection. Gary's brain went into combat mode. He locked eyes on the driver's door, buckled his seatbelt, and floored it. *I should've rented a fullsize.*

*****

Pavilax, after holding his demonic enemies at bay with angelic wind, now launched himself at the assassins' protectors. He struck them at the very moment Gary struck their vehicle.

*****

Cortney heard a crash that could only mean one thing. *Dad!* She bolted toward the sound. When she rounded the corner in a full sprint, she saw her dad struggling with Karen in the street.

It wasn't much of a struggle. Karen whirled Gary around and threw him from the street, all the way to the lawn of the northeast corner house. Then, exceeding Cortney's elevated level of expectation, Karen leaped what must have been eight feet in the air and landed across Gary's chest.

Young men were starting to stare from the porches of Fraternity Row as the dazed driver emerged from the passenger side of the SUV.
    "Nothing to see here, folks. Just a fender-bender."

It looked even to Cortney, that Karen was helping Gary, as she choked him. Instinctively, she yelled:
    "Hey! Karen! I have your little box."

Karen got off Gary and ambled toward Cortney like a wounded wolf to a housecat. Her face twisted into a sinister grim.
    "Give it to me!"

Her dad was wobbling to his feet, when the Blonde man punched him.

Now what? Fight. Cortney slipped into her Tae Kwon Do fighting stance. Karen laughed and rushed her. Cortney timed the sweep perfectly. Karen landed on her head. *That should do it.*

But Karen got up laughing, and walked right threw two round-house kicks. Cortney was out of room, and out of time. Karen's grip felt like two vices on Cortney's shoulders. Putrid saliva dripped from the corners of her mouth as she bare teeth towards Cortney's neck. She remembered what Brice did to Stocker. *Will it hurt? God don't let it hurt.*

    "Hey! Over here, you bitch!"
    Dad? The blonde guy was on his knees. Gary held the puzzle box over his head.
    "Is this what you're looking for?"

Cortney hit the concrete hard, after being tossed aside like a rag doll. The blonde caught Gary from behind with a kidney punch. Gary dropped the box and turned to face the attack. It seemed important for Gary to tell the man that someone else knew his secret.
    "We know who you are," Gary almost yelled. "We know what you're

planning."

Karen raced for the puzzle box. But a winded Gizmo picked it up first, and pitched it. Cortney watched it arc, slightly. Nerdy Trevor actually snagged it, like a shortstop catching a line drive. *Wow!* Karen ran for Trevor, who threw the box to Cortney. *He can throw too?*

Three of them played 'Monkey in the Middle' with Karen, while the crowd grew around the fistfight between her dad and the other driver. It was almost fun to watch Karen's panic. It seemed just a simple case of road rage.

Gary was outpunching the blonde. *Not bad for an old man.*
 "Nadia's not gonna like this," Gary said, with a jab – jab - cross.
Out of nowhere, the other driver put a tricky judo move on Gary and slammed him on his back. It *had* to hurt. Gary didn't get up. The man went back to the vehicle.

Karen was fast, but she was no match for the three-way juggling act. The game ended with a muffled thud…and a hole in Karen's forehead. The silencer was still smoking when the assassin shot her twice in the chest. Karen crumpled to her knees and fell over on her side.

People ran screaming, from the man with the long handgun. Trevor and Gizmo disappeared with the crowds. Cortney didn't run. She couldn't – not with her father lying at the man's feet.
 "They have your puzzle box," Cortney proclaimed, as if the man cared.
 "They can keep it. I have you," the man countered, wiping blood from his nose. "I believe this man is your father. Get in the van or I will kill him."

He pointed the gun at Gary's head.
 "Ok, ok, just – please, don't hurt him."
 "Get in."

The door was still open. Cortney got in the passenger seat. *Don't get up, Dad. Please don't get up.* The man came through the back door and climbed around her, to the driver's seat. Cortney hadn't noticed that the engine was still running. She saw Gizmo in the passenger-side rearview as they sped away.

*****

One demon's dust laid sprinkled on Karen's twitching body. The other submitted to Pavilax's chokehold, as Pavilax merged their essences with the roof of the escaping vehicle.

CHAPTER 30

Gary lumbered to his feet with stars swimming around his aching head. College-aged men stood in clusters nearby. Wailing sirens told Gary that police would be on the scene in minutes. The SUV was gone. His dizzied eyes scanned for his daughter. But he couldn't focus.

"Where is she?" He asked when Gizmo's face congealed in front of him. Gizmo showed him his cell phone. The license plate of the black SUV was at the center.

"Sorry Mister Landau. We didn't know what to do."

Karen lay twitching in the street not far away, with tarry colored ooze leaking from her forehead. The back of her head fared worse.

"*He* did that?" Gary asked, already knowing the answer.

"Yeah," Gizmo answered and apologized again. "We didn't know what to do."

Karen's eyes were open. She should have been dead.

"Naaadia...Nadia...Na...Na...Nadia."

Gary knelt over her.

"Where's Nadia?"

Karen's eyes searched for an answer.

"Where is she, Karen?"

Her body convulsed.

Gary looked up.

"Who's got the puzzle box?"

Trevor handed it to him.

"Do you want this, Karen?"

Karen's eyes widened in her necrotized face. And she reached up.

"Uh-uh," Gary toyed with her. "Tell me where to find Nadia and I'll open it for you."

"Belarus?" Gary asked.

Karen nodded and clutched at the box.

"Does she have the missiles?"

She nodded.

Police cars closed in from two directions. *Cut to the chase, Gary. These are Soviet Special Operatives.*

"Where's your extraction point?"

The living corpse shook its ugly head.

"I don't …know…I…"

"Sir – back away please."

Times up. Gary smiled at Karen's pain. And backed away making sure she saw the puzzle box in his hand. As responders surrounded their dying patient, Karen sceamed like a banshee. Gary took pleasure in knowing she was in a very special brand of agony.

"Mister Landau?"

Gary's mind was in the driver's head. *They can't be more than a mile from here. Gotta find them before he ditch's the truck.*

"Mister Landau?"

It was Gizmo.

"My phone. Can I have my phone."

"Oh – right. Hold on."

Gary sent the picture to Jeff, with a text: 'FOX 1 run this 911. Send results to my phone.' Then he deleted the message, and the picture.

"Here you go."

Gizmo looked surprised.

"What about the police?"

"Go home, son. I'll take it from here."

"Is that your car, sir?" *Campus Police?*

"What about Cortney?" Trevor asked

"He won't hurt her," Gary whispered. "She's a bargaining chip. The cops 'll only get her killed. Keep your mouths shut and go home."

"Sir, can you step over here please?"

A large, uniformed Black man looked down at him. Gary recognized his military baring, instantly.

"I'm officer Roberts – Campus Police. Is that your car?"

"Yes. It's a rental."

"Your name please?"

"Gary Landau?"

"Mister Landau, do you know that young woman lying in the street?"

Come on bro – they're getting away. If I tell him – damn.

"My daughter knows her."

Roberts eyed the paramedics. He gave Trevor and Gizmo a knowing glance.

"Mister Landau, where is your daughter now?"

"Whoa – hold it right there. Cortney didn't shoot her."

"Then who did?"

Ok, this is getting way too complicated. The back of Gary's head was bleeding. That would be his play. He wiped his hand in the blood and feigned dizziness.

"Sir – are you hurt?"

Gary nodded.

"Are you in need of medical attention?"

Gary capitalized on the statement, taking the lead in the conversation.

"Yeah. Just let me get my bag out of the car. I'll give you my statement on the way to the hospital."

"Ok," Roberts said, and unsnapped his holster. "But make it slow. And keep your hands where I can see em."

Gary answered the obvious question.

"The other driver shot the girl. I'll explain on the way."

Gary eased his laptop case, and the way too warm winter coat, out of the back seat. *This is taking way too long.*

"This way," Officer Roberts beckoned, with *elite* military baring.

Gary got in the front passenger seat. There was no way he was going to commandeer this guy's vehicle.

"I'm gonna ask you just one more time, Mister Landau. Where's Cortney."

There was his opening.

"I never said her name was Cortney."

Sirens blared from all directions, with different Doppler shifts; meaning they were headed in different directions. There was surely and APB out on the SUV.

"Your daughter confided in me yesterday, that the girl in the street was connected to a vicious attack."

Gary took the bull by the horns.

"You were Special Forces, right?"

"Army Ranger," the man half smiled. "Does it still show?"

"It jumps off the page, Brother. We have to catch up to them before they switch vehicles."

Gary held his breath. *This has to work.*

"They?"

"He's got Cortney."

"Which way?"

"Take the next left."

Roberts gunned it. *It worked.*

"You figure he's headed for extraction?"

"Exactly, but that crunched truck is way too easy to spot. He'll be looking for another..."

And BOOM! Gary didn't get the word 'vehicle' out of his mouth. Roberts knew what to do.

"Two miles west. I'm on it. You CIA or something?"

Gary's heart pounded with a fresh surge of adrenalin.

"I'm a librarian," he huffed.

Roberts gave him a funny look and powered toward the explosion adding his siren to the others.

CHAPTER 31

With all the other high-profile crimes in the area, Roberts was first to arrive on the scene. The SUV was fully engulfed, in the far corner of a crowded grocery store parking lot.

"Mister Landau?"

"Call me Gary. Don't worry, she's not in there. She's not expendable."

"Yet," Roberts added. "Smell that?" He asked.

"Yeah – C4," Gary answered. "This guy is Soviet Ops."

"How do you..." Roberts was about to ask.

"I fell for his Soviet Ops judo flip. No time to wait to see who's missing a car. He's headed for the airport."

Again, Roberts knew the drill.

"Van Nuys would be my guess. It's close. And small."

"I agree. Go!"

Gary fished his phone out of his coat pocket. The message from Jeff read: 'SSOPs.' *Soviet Ops. I knew it.*

"Gary?"

"Officer?"

"It's Joe. Call me Joe. You gotta fill me in, man. What the hell is all this about?"

There was no delicate or diplomatic filter to explain it – no way to put spin on it.

"Vampires, Joe."

To Gary's surprise, Joe answered:

"I was afraid you were gonna say that."

Joe cut across lanes and swerved onto the northbound 405 freeway.

"Vampires with intercontinental-ballistic nuclear missiles."

Joe weaved through morning traffic with a license to speed.

"Funny, Gary. I believe everything except the librarian part. Really – who are you?"

"I work at the Library of Congress – Russian Studies Division. I'm a Russian weapon's expert. I was a fighter pilot; shot down and held hostage as a cold war bargaining chip."

"Ok, that makes sense. ETA twelve minutes."

"Go straight to the private side of the airport. Why aren't you surprised about the Vampires?"

"My friend, Brenda, is stuck in the Isolation Ward with your daughter's friend, Stocker. I saw their friend, Brice, bite Stocker in the neck yesterday before he was put down by police. Stocker's heart stopped early this morning."

"And?"

"He's still alive," Joe said and paused. "What's your play?"

"Simple hostage swap," Gary told him. "Me for her."

Joe killed his siren at the Van Nuys Boulevard offramp.

"Without a siren, they can't be more than five minutes ahead of us," Gary instructed:

"There'll be a Gulfstream Gee Five, waiting for them."

"How come you know that?"

"It's the only private jet with range enough for a Transatlantic flight."

Joe gunned it and made (or ran) every light between the freeway and the airport. And sure enough, a blue and white, twin engine private jet taxied away from a car with the doors left open.

"There they are, Joe."

"Damn! Are we too late? Should I cut em off?"

"No time. They're not gonna wait for clearance."

Gary pulled his laptop case from the back seat. It opened more like a briefcase. He lifted the screen and it powered up. He pulled a headset from a zippered compartment and plugged into a jack on the side of the overly thick keyboard console. He took a stub antenna from another compartment, uncoiled the cable, and jacked it in.

"Stop here, Joe"

"Here?"

"Right here," Gary said, with military finality.

Then he let down his window and put the antenna on the roof with a magnetic click. Joe just watched while Gary typed in a frequency, a SRAM code, and hit send. 'Acknowledged' scrolled up the screen.

Gary's friend and former wingman, Air Force Colonel James Curtis, was on day two of a forty-eight hour shift. James was the Communications Officer aboard AWACS West Two; an Advanced Warning and Control Systems aircraft, circling over the Pacific Ocean between Hawaii and the U.S. Mainland. His own boss had no idea that Gary had the equipment, or the capability, to do what he was about to do.

"SRAM Code two, four, niner, X-ray, Foxtrot, Romeo – requesting scrambled clearance on VOR one-twenty-three point nine megahertz FSK. Please confirm."

Joe stared, wide-eyed, as Gary waited for confirmation.

"Challenge code eight, eight, one, Tango, Echo, November."

"Fox One," Gary answered. "Singin in the rain."

"Go ahead, Colonel Landau."

"Eyes on SSOPs Bogie. Blue on white Gulfstream Gee five. Tail number delta, delta, one, four, seven, seven, six. Hold one."

Gary waited for the loud Gulfstream engines to tear past him on the runway.

"Bogey, carrying a Christmas Package, just took off from Van Nuys airport, bound due west…watching for coarse correction. Watching…watching…turning south. Probably headed out of U.S. airspace. Repeat – Bogey has a Christmas Package."

"Copy Fox One. We're on it. delta, delta, one, four, seven, seven, six. With a Christmas Package. But you know we'll need proper authorization."

"Curt?"

"Go ahead, Gary."

"The package is my daughter, Cortney."

"Copy that, Gary. We'll track her to egress."

"Copy that. And since we're barkin' up a tall tree. Can you send me a quick ride home?"

"Only for you, Gary. Anything else?"

"Yeah, Curt. Give Beau a heads up."

"Roger that, Fox One. West Two out."

Joe's mouth was hanging open.

"Who the hell are you, man?"

"I already told you, Joe. I'm just a librarian. You can drop me off here. My rides on the way. Just tell em you took my statement in the hospital parking lot."

"How will I know… I mean what if…"

Gary understood.

"If things go well, you won't hear anything about the nukes."

"And if it doesn't?"

"You'll know."

"Um, Gary?"

"Hold on. I gotta make a call."

Gary had Jeff on speed dial.

"Hey Jeff…No, they took her. Find Uri. I'll call you later."

He hung up.

"Yeah, Joe. What is it?"

"I'm gonna need to see your driver's license."

CHAPTER 32

Stocker stared at the ceiling, covered with ice packs, as a quarantined suited Brenda set up the ultrasound apparatus. Two other nurses (Phyliss and Carlos) fiddled with tubes and wires attached to various parts of his body. It was finally sinking in. He was on a one-way trip to a ghoulish end.

He looked down at his feet. They looked more like stone than flesh. He almost asked for a mirror, but knew he wouldn't be able to handle what he saw. Horrified at the thought of what he must look like, he touched his face. His still heart sank. He couldn't feel a thing; not with his fingers *or* his face. He had only one purpose – one passion or hope.
"More Blood!"

A quarantined orderly named Mike, nodded in a chair between Stocker's bed and the door.
"What? What time is it?" Mike asked groggily.
As Doctor Tobias Hardyway came through the door, Mike reached to wipe his mouth, but his hand hit the quarantine hood faceplate instead.

*****

"Mike, since you're not busy sleeping, how about calling the cafeteria? Order breakfast for ten…"
"Make that twelve," a stranger corrected.
"What? Who are you? And who let you in here?"
"Cynthia Guinn – C.D.C. epidemiologist. My partner is suiting up in the airlock."
"Just in time then. I'm doctor Hardyway – vascular surgeon. This is the

third Ultrasound, in twenty-four hours. His condition is deteriorating…"

Mike was still standing there.

"Breakfast for twelve, Mike. And call the blood bank. We're running low on O-positive. Get them to send up ten liters," Tobias ordered, dismissively, and turned his attention back to Cynthia. "There are oxygen hungry parasites multiplying in his blood stream at an alarming rate…"

"And the other's?" Cynthia interrupted.

"Three police officers and one nosey reporter - all screened - no sign of infection."

"Then why…" Cynthia motioned toward Carmen Murphy, who stood just outside the door. "…is *she* still here."

"She's supposed to be in her own room under observation," Brenda's baffled voice came through the audio filtration channels.

"How's he doing?" Carmen asked, as Tobias examined the settings on the ultrasound display.

A man, who must have been Cynthia's partner overheard.

"You come with me," he told Carmen, and helped her away from the door."

Cynthia took Stocker's chart off the bed hooks.

"Go ahead, doctor. I'm listening."

"His heart stopped three hours ago."

Cynthia didn't seem surprised.

"His temperature is down to eighty-four. Respiration, ten shallow breaths per minute. Let's just see what we can see. This won't hurt, Stocker. Just try and relax."

"Oh God, Doctor. What's happening to me? Why am I so hot? All I can think of is blood. Can I have some more.?"

"We'll see. After I examine you."

Tobias smeared the probe into the gel, searching for an image of Stocker's heart.

"I can't see anything," he muttered. "His skin is hardening, it's tough as leather.

"Try decreasing the frequency," Brenda offered.

They all looked at her; even Stocker. Tobias raised an eyebrow, but nodded his approval.

Brenda rolled the cursor over to the frequency display and typed 1 Mhz, decreasing it from 4. It worked.

"The cardiac tissue is dying," Tobias commented. "Get him over on his right side."

Phylis and Carlos tried to roll Stocker over, but his restrained left leg stopped them short.

"Take off the restraints."

With the restraints undone, the two rolled Stocker over to his right side. Tobias slid the probe around his chest, from armpit to sternum, shooting sound waves between his second and third ribs. His comments were directed at Cynthia.

"See here. The right atrium, the left pulmonary artery…and the aorta . . . all still alive."

He moved the probe back and forth between the ribs.

"The vessels between the lungs and heart are blocked. See that small hole?"

"I see it," Cynthia answered. "A passage from the right atrium, through the left pulmonary vein, and into the aorta."

"His circulatory system has been re-engineered," Tobias expounded.

"Re-engineered?" Brenda asked.

"By the parasites," Cynthia answered.

She's done her homework. "They're changing him," Tobias continued. "Reforming him to suit their physiology. Roll him over on his left side."

As Stocker was rolled over the freezing ice packs his sad eyes met Tobias's.

"What's happening to me?"

No one said a word as Tobias thought.

"You've been abducted…" he said finally, "…from the inside out, by microscopic pirates."

Cynthia's partner stuck his hooded face around the doorjamb.

"Head's up team," he said, as he struggled to keep nosey Carmen out of the room. "We have another one on the way up. Gunshot wounds to the head. Still alive."

Cynthia took charge of the exchange.

"Prep another room."

"An operating room," Tobias elaborated.

"And, Andy," Cynthia continued. "*She* (referring to Carmen) can't be allowed to leave. Keep her off the phone too."

*****

Gary rang Judy's Price's Baltimore doorbell at 7:45pm. She answered it, in a hurried frenzy.

"Really, Gary? I ought to fire you right here and now. What the hell did you do out there? General Beauregard ripped me a new one."

"They took my daughter, Judy. I had no choice."

"It's your own fault. You shouldn't have gotten involved."

"I was *already* involved when they attacked Cortney's friend."

Gary's war medals, and tall tales of daring do, always seemed to rustle Judy's feathers. She'd spent her adult life behind a desk. She didn't invite Gary in.

"We need to talk, Judy. You gonna let me in, or what?"

"I wasn't planning on it."

Dressed for travel, she grudgingly stepped aside.

"Make it quick. Our flight leaves in two hours."

"That's why I'm here, Judy. I want your authorization to join the negotiations in Minsk."

She laughed and turned to the couch, to smoosh her overstuffed suitcase.

"You want my authorization," she mocked. "You're no diplomat. You're a brash and arrogant…"

"I'm your Russian Weapons Expert. How can you even consider not taking me?"

"Because," she turned to him. "You have no tack, no filter, and no patience. General Beauregard agrees. We've got a handle on this. I gave his attaché the underground coordinates to…"

Gary exploded.

"*You* gave them coordinates? *You* gave? *I* figured out where they're hiding those missiles. You couldn't find your way out of a barn…"

Judy held up a finger. *Oops.*

"See how you are, Gary? And that's my point. Jeff was there with you when you figured it out. You didn't even give *him* credit. It always has to be *your* show. And that's why you're not coming."

Gary knew he'd gone too far.

"Judy, please? They have my daughter."

Judy shook her head and showed Gary the door.

"Get out, Gary!"

Gary tucked tail and walked. When he cleared the threshold, Judy added:

"And by the way…you're fired. You can clean out your desk when I get back."

Gary's laptop was buzzing when he opened his car door. He opened it to find a low signal strength warning. A SRAM Code appeared when he deployed the stubby antenna. He answered with a challenge code. The encrypted transponder hidden in his laptop broke squelch.

"West Two — dancing in the rain."

"Fox One reads you five by five. What-a-ya got, Curt?"

"Bogey entered Canadian airspace at eighteen hundred hours, GMT. Landed briefly in Quebec. No cooperation from Canadian government. Left Quebec at twenty-oh-five GMT. Currently midway across the North Atlantic. And Gary?"

"Yeah Curt?"

"My authorization was revoked. I've been ordered to stand down."

"By who?" Gary asked, but he already knew who it was.

"General Beauregard."

"Thanks, Curt. I owe you one. Just one question."

"Go ahead."

"Are they on a course for Minsk?"

"Affirmative, Fox One. West Two Out."

Gary cursed under his breath, all the way to the Library. Ann Li was waiting with Jeff at the Second Street, night entrance. Jeff held the door.

"What'd she say?"

"She fired me."

"We figured she would," Ann admitted, and held up a manila folder. "I've got the latest satellite pass. Come on."

Jeff secured the door with a shake of the long, bar of a handle.

"I've got us two seats booked on the 2:45 out of Ronald Reagan."

"Two seats? What about Uri?"

"He has his own resources."

Six librarian footsteps echoed through silent halls. Jeff took a right toward the first staircase.

"We're set up down in 4-E."

Gary stopped at the stairs.

"I'll take those, Ann. You should go home, while you still have plausible deniability."

Ann's heels clicked down the stairs.

"I'm in this up to my eyeballs, Gary. No way I'm leaving until there's a solid plan to get Cortney back. I hate this job, anyway."

CHAPTER 33

Arlington County, Virginia
Friday, 20 January

Gary slipped and slid, on the freshly salted, icy Pentagon parking lot. Between his library credentials and his Air Force Reserve clearances, he made it all the way to General Beauregard's ready room, carrying his laptop case. He was challenged at the door by armed guards, but Beauregard let him through.

"I ought'a have you arrested for that stunt you pulled yesterday. You just never learn, do you? Is that the mobile unit you checked out of Langley yesterday morning?"

"They sent a hitman after my daughter, Sir. There wasn't any time to go through proper channels."

"Sargent, relieve him of that equipment."
Gary handed it over.

"It hasn't been out my sight, General. I needed to cover every eventuality. I know where she is. I should be at those negotiations."

"Not on your life, Colonel!" The general bellowed. "Those are sensitive talks, and…"

"Goddammit, Beau, they have my daughter! Authorize a ground assault, and I'll lead them straight…"

"Don't you *dare* come in here barking orders at me. Those people are nuclear terrorists. I don't care if they had my own dear mother held hostage. If those talks fall through, I'm going to rain holy hell on that bunker complex. Now get the hell out of my ready room."

"I've known you since nineteen seventy-three, Beau!" Gary shouted as he walked toward his former boss. "We go all the way back to Viet Nam! You were just a captain then – a captain for Christ sakes! Now you stand there with all those stars on your shoulder, full of self-righteous justification, and tell me you're not gonna help me. I ought'a kick your ass right now, you son of a bitch!"

By the time Gary finished, he was nose to nose with the general. Beauregard didn't give an inch. He didn't even blink.

"You see, Gary – that was always your problem; always a hothead, never seeing the big picture. That's why I'm a general, and you're in the Reserves!"

"Sergeants! Get this man out of here! See him all the way to his vehicle!"

Gary felt two sets of hands snatch him backward.

"Gary," the general added as Gary was dragged away. "You're a good man. That's the only reason you're not in handcuffs."

The two burly sergeants marched Gary away from the checkpoint, just as a large contingency of Pentagon security burst through the outer doors.

Gary was silent as they took him up the bunker elevator and out to the inner ring, where they caught a service elevator up to the ground floor. Security guards joined the procession as they went.

"What lot are you parked in?" A voice came from behind Gary.

"T!" Gary spat.

"This way then," he heard, as he was jerked to the left.

By the time they had traversed the radial arm and out to the outer ring of the building there were two dozen security officers. Curious glances caught Gary's icy stare as they passed by Pentagon staffers. Another handful of officers met them at the exit. It was so crowded that they had a hard time squeezing through the door.

*****

"Shit, I knew it!" Jeff said into his cell phone as he watched the throng approaching the car. "Okay, Uri. Gary's on the way now; him and about two dozen security guards. The usual place. Room fourteen. If we leave right now, we'll be there in forty minutes."

Gary's car was parked at the end of a row. And the horde had no problem all crowding near it. They snatched the driver's door open and slammed Gary down in the seat. Jeff looked over from the passenger seat as Gary reached for the keys, already in the ignition.

"Jeff, I swear if you say one…" Gary stopped short.

"That was Uri on the phone, Gary. He booked us on the...what? What's wrong?"

*****

Gary started the car and slowly pulled out into the aisle.

"Jeff," Gary said slowly, as he pulled ahead of a man running in the next aisle.

"Jeff, that's him. THAT'S THE GUY!"

"What guy?"

"THAT'S THE BASTARD THAT KIDNAPPED CORTNY!"

Curiously, the Blonde man didn't run away. Gary put his car in park and jumped out. Jeff followed suit. The guy just stood there with his hands up. Gary tackled him anyway.

"WHERE IS SHE?" Gary yelled, and raised his fist.

"No need for that. I'll tell you everything."

Gary punched him anyway. The blonde just laid there and took it.

"Tell me where she is!"

"By now," the blonde tried to sit up. "She is with Nadia."

Gary considered bashing the man's head on the ice.

"Give me a reason to let you live."

Jeff intervened.

"Whoa, Gary. Hold on. I think the man has something to tell us."

"He'd better spit it out then."

"Let em up before we draw attention."

The blonde stood, and spat blood.

"I can keep your daughter alive."

Gary was about to punch him again.

"And I can help you get her back."

"And why would you do that?"

"Because *I* am in more trouble than *you* are. Call me Peter. Nadia has put a price on my head. I slipped away, while we were refueling in Quebec. I flew here to help you. You must believe that."

"And what do you want in return?" Jeff asked.

Peter nodded in submission.

"For you to make sure Nadia is dead."

CHAPTER 34

Washington D.C.

Gary was peeking out the curtain when Uri drove up to the motel. The motel handyman was salting down the icy parking lot from a ten-pound bag of rock salt. He shook his head to himself, as yet a forth man approached the door of Room 14. Uri reached out to knock, but Gary opened the door before his knuckles made contact. The two men stared at each other for a long time through the open door, and then embraced and kissed each other on both cheeks.

The handyman must have misinterpreted the nostalgic interlude, and chuckled to himself as he threw a handful of salt on the ground. *It's not what you think.* Gary was about to explain, when:
"For God's sake, let him in, Gary. It's freezing out there," Jeff's voice boomed.
Gary stepped aside and Uri came in.
"It has been a long time. Much too long, my friend," Uri said to Gary in a heavy Russian accent. He then looked at Jeff and smiled.
"Jefferson, it is good to see you also. Now, tell me what is so important that you…"

Uri's expression changed when he saw Peter.
"What is this man doing here?"
"He's here to help," Gary answered grudgingly.
"I doubt that very much," Uri said without taking his eyes off Peter. "Do you two know who this is?"
"We know he's Soviet Special Ops," Jeff answered. "Says his name is Peter."

"Not just any Peter. Not just SSOPS. This man is Petrov Brume – The Sweeper. He only comes to kill. How many dead so far?"

Peter also knew Uri.

"Only one, Uri. How long have you been hiding here, right under their noses?"

"I have made peace with my past. But why should any of us trust a heartless killer?"

"When there is a shark after the barracuda, the barracuda and the bass become brothers."

"Until the barracuda offers the bass to the shark."

Gary let it soak in. *Uri's right, but...*

"My daughter is held hostage by his boss."

"Nadia Romanov?"

"So, you know her *real* name. Then you also know where she's hiding."

"In the Romanov stronghold, of course. No need for us to trust *him*."

"He has friends on the inside," Gary said, then looked at Peter. "*They* keep Cortney alive. *We* kill Nadia, before *she* kills Peter.

Jeff took a seat in a plain wooden chair.

"Undoubtedly you've heard about the missile crisis in Belarus?" He said, motioning toward the other empty chair.

Uri sat down.

"The government has kept it from the people, but yes, I still have my sources. What does this have to do with Gary's family?"

"The same faction that stole the missiles killed a boy near Cortney's college campus. Cortney got too close. They sent Peter to shut her up," Jeff explained. "But Gary got in his way."

"Bastard put Cortney on his escape plane," Gary added.

"I had no choice," Peter explained. "The situation was out of control. They know who you are, Colonel Landau. A Central Intelligence Agent, posing as a librarian. They expect your government to negotiate on her behalf, just long enough for them to..."

Uri cut him off.

"Are they holding her in the stronghold?"

Jeff answered.

"Yes. And Gary has a plan to get her out."

"Wait a moment, my friend," Uri said. "If what you say is true, you know as well as I that most of Eastern Belarus was laid waste by fallout from the Chernobyl explosion."

"You're right, Uri," Gary cut in. "And this huge underground bunker is located in the hottest zone."

"So how is it that you think they even *survive*, let alone *operate* in that area?"

"They must be wearing radiation suits and operating under the cover of the fallout to keep everybody else out," Gary answered.

Peter motioned to be heard.

"Some of them, like the girl I shot in California, don't have to wear radiation suits. Her kind are Valmpir..."

"A myth," Uri insisted.

Peter ignored him.

"They thrive on radiation. *They* sabotaged the reactor at Chernobyl. And Queen Nadia wants to turn your country into a nuclear wasteland. Your citizens will survive in pockets. But they will be herded like cattle. And kept fat until they are slaughtered for blood."

"He's right, Uri," Gary agreed. "I saw one with my own eyes."

"Surely the U.S. military will get your daughter out . . ."

"No. They won't. You remember Colonel Beauregard?" Gary asked.

"Of course. He was your wing commander when you brought me out. He was hawk of all hawks."

Gary nodded.

"Yeah, well he's a three-star general now, and he's running the whole show. He's on the button, and he'll nuke the whole sight if they so much as aim one of those missiles. He won't allow troops in, because they'll interfere with a preemptive strike,"

"How are you certain of this?"

"Because I asked him," Gary answered. "We sent a diplomatic team to Belarus yesterday. Negotiations begin tomorrow morning. They're hoping to orchestrate a peaceful solution, but what they refuse to understand is that Belarussian government officials and military officers have been bought off."

"Hell, our boss is even there, and she won't listen to us either," Jeff added.

"This sounds like a State Department matter. Which are you; State Department, or CIA?" Uri asked.

"Neither – we're librarians," Gary said. "The point is they're not making any progress. The Belarussian government is denying any ties to the terrorists, and when the diplomats come out...we go to DEFCON Three."

"Then what do you propose, my friend?" Uri asked.

"That's why I called you. I have a plan, but we'll need a Soviet MIG," Gary said flatly.

"Steal another MIG, you say? I'm an American citizen now, where would I get a MIG?"

"Like you said, you still have your sources," Jeff said from across the table.

"Listen," Uri said, "I owe you my life. You brought me out when I defected. You flew your eagle right beside me, right through the firestorm . . ."

"He also shot down a MIG that had you in its sights," Jeff interjected.

"And I gave your government the MIG in return!" Uri said, pounding a fist on the table.

Gary walked over and placed a hand on each of Uri's shoulders, and spoke in Russian.

"This is not for America, Uri. It's for me. They've got my kid!"
Uri lowered his head.

"The cold war is over, my friend. This time I would not be a defector, only a thief!"

Silence waited for Uri's answer.

"Alright," Uri said finally, "What intelligence do you have so far?"

"Their leader is female," Gary said. "She's known as Nadia Roman. We have a picture, but not much more. It seems she has no traceable history, beyond a few years ago. We think Nadia controls vast amounts of money, though we haven't tracked down a single account. She's known to have connections to the Belarussian underground, as well as the government, and the military.

Uri nodded, as Jeff took over

"We think she's headquartered in the underground complex. The structure was built in the late fifteen-hundreds, under the secret order of Ivan the Terrible. It was intended to be a royal refuge for his entire court, if he was ever overthrown.

He had slaves dig tunnels between existing coal mines. They dug in secrecy for four years, eventually removing most of the coal and increasing the size of the complex to about a city block. The water table stopped them from burrowing below about fifty feet. When the excavation was completed, the bastard had them all killed; hundreds of them.

Though the shelter was never used, each successive ruler used clandestine labor to improve upon the initial effort. Peter the Great added a complex drainage system. Catherine the Great sent in builders and craftsmen of all sorts, making the place livable, by royal standards.

The workers were always killed. By the eighteen-hundreds, the facility was palatial, and was actually considered for occupancy by more than one of the remaining tsars. Nicholas, the last Tsar, had gone so far as to move his family keepsakes into the lair, with provisions for a year's seclusion.

They never got to use it of course. Their plans were leaked, and the family was taken into custody before they could escape. In nineteen-forty-eight, Nadia married a man named Vladimir Roman…"

"We call him The Old One," Peter elaborated. "He lives, only for Nadia."

Gary picked up where Jeff left off.

"We found information in an Italian diary written by a man named Leonardo. Him and his future wife, Madip, were on an expedition with this *same* man when they were ambushed by Valmpir. That's the word he used. This *same* Vladimir commandeered a tug after being bitten. His transformation sounds just like the girl I saw in California with my own eyes.

When we researched Russian accounts, they said that the sickness turned its victims into cannibals. We found similar stories about monsters in Belarus. Monsters that live off the blood of others . . ."

"It's all true," Peter said. "Let's get on with it. I will tell you how to get inside."

Uri was pensive.

"It could be that he is a double agent, assigned to keep an eye on Gary, and confound his efforts; a common SSOP tactic."

Gary and Jeff looked at each other, neither man able to rule out the possibility.

"I wouldn't put it past him," Gary admitted. "He could tip them off, once I'm in the air."

"Then you are going to need a wing man," Uri stated.

"Even if we could get our hands on two planes, who's gonna…" Gary started, then realized what Uri was saying. "I can't ask that much of you, Uri."

"You did it for me in eighty-four. The two of us stand a better chance than you alone. I will help you get the planes, and then I will help you to get your daughter. And you trust this killer to get us in?"

Gary and Jeff hadn't discussed their Ops Plan with Peter.

"Jeff," take him outside while I fill Uri in."

Gary waited until Jeff closed the door, then unrolled maps from a tube.

"We have diagrams of the facility as it evolved over the centuries. We overlaid satellite photos of the area and we think we see an entrance; the same one Peter told us about. He doesn't know we have the same intel. Peter showed us the transceiver station. We'll take it out first, to cut off radio communications, then the transformer to cut off power.

"There's a large cavern, capable of hiding the mobile launchers. If we hit it before they roll out, our job will be easy. Then I'll blow off the back door and punch out, while you keep them distracted, I'll go in on foot and get Cortney. Jeff should be at the southern border by then. If you punch out near the border, he can pick you up. I'll bring Cortney out, and we'll wait for you and Jeff at this river.

We're expecting better resolution on the next satellite pass. We hope it'll provide more leverage." Gary paused. "And speaking of leverage, I took the liberty of making up this grocery list."

Gary handed Uri a stack of papers from the map tube. Uri browsed the list, then looked up.

"You're kidding, right? You think this stuff is just lying around? You want air-to-ground missiles with four different tracking modes, and a helmet-sighting mode? You want a broadband signal-jamming module with, what is this, 'acquire and jam-on transmitter'? I never heard of that. What the hell is that? And full stealth coatings?"

"I assure you, all of these items are standard options these days," Gary told him.

"You have quite a comprehensive package here. Where are you getting all this information?"

"From the greatest research center on earth," Gary said proudly.

"The CIA?"

"No, not the CIA," Gary said with a smile. "The United States Library of Congress."

Gary looked back at the motel door, wondering what they'd to with Peter. Uri must have red his mind.

"Wait here, I have something for *him* in my truck."
Gary hurried behind Uri, knowing from a bloody past that Uri would have no problem snuffing Peter.

"Slow down, Uri."

"Trust me, old friend."

Uri popped his truck with his remote key.

"No, Uri. We're not gonna…"
Gary stopped in mid-sentence, when Uri pulled a bottle from his trunk. Uri laughed.

"Did you think I would kill him?"
Gary loosened his collar.

"I wouldn't put it passed you."

"It's only *Wodka*. Follow my lead."

CHAPTER 35

Cortney fought her way up, though levels of consciousness. This was surely a dream; vampires, kidnapping, and a seemingly endless flight. Through her fog, she was sure she'd be given another shot. *I have to wake up.*
"No. Please – no more."

Something was different this time. A murky layer. A transparent gate. *What is this?* Gurgling voices sharpened to clarity.
"...Nadia...*something...something*...Nadia..."
They're Russian.
"...Peter...*something...something*...Gary Landau...librarian. Hahaha."
Oh God – Dad – Stocker – Oh God.

I'm falling. Down, down through a rocky shaft. As orientation returned she realized that the masonry shaft was really a lighted tunnel. She was being dragged. Dragged by two hooded men, dressed in canvas coveralls.
"Hey! Let me go!"
"Can you walk?"
"Yes."
They helped her to her feet – like friends.
"Come. We must hurry."

Her vision never quite cleared. Her skin was irritated; rubbed the wrong way.
"What is this?"
"Radiation suit. Keep you safe. Hurry."

The three of them wore dill green radiation suits, with mesh and glass visors, like the door on a microwave oven. One of the men was silent. He carried a box, strapped over one shoulder.

"What radiation?"

"Chernobyl very close. This way."

Her friendly captures marched her down an ancient stairway leading to a dank underworld. Bones littered the uneven rocky floor. Chills shot down Cortney's spine. *What is this place?* Mud filled every depression. Water dripped from the ceiling like the first drops of a storm. She had no urge to run. Where would she go?

"Where are you taking me?"

They passed a rusty grate of a cell door on the right. Then another on the left.

"This looks like a…"

"Queen Nadia's dungeon."

"You're not going to leave me here?"

"This one for you. Get in."

The thick, rusty, grate of a door creaked and screeched on its hinges. Cortney panicked, but they held her fast. The second man finally spoke, in perfect English.

"Don't struggle. If you tear the suit, you'll die. Do yourself a favor and go inside."

"You must be the good cop," Cortney said sarcastically.

He unshouldered the box and tossed it in the cell.

"Two days rations. Eat only when you must. When you open a can, unsnap your visor, and gobble it down. Remember the radiation."

"And what happens after two days?"

The guy with the Russian accent pushed her in.

"Will all be over in two days. Smile."

A light flashed in her face before the door slammed. *A picture? He took my picture?* As he struggled to turn the rusty lock, she pictured the key breaking off…just before it broke off. The good cop lingered, as the Russian walked away laughing.

"You weren't supposed to end like this," he whispered. "I'm sorry."

And he walked away. And then he walked back. Cortney was about to beg for her life."

"Shhh. I hear your father is a resourceful man. I'll tell him where to find you."

Cortney shook the bars.

"Huh? What's that supposed to mean?"

"Shhh."

She was alone. Locked in a long-forgotten cage, somewhere between hell and earth. Terror pulsed with her every heartbeat. She closed her eyes and pictured her father breaking down the door. *He'll find me. Please, God help him find me.*

Sooner than her prayer was complete, the Russian's laugh turned to screams. Cortney pressed her visor against the bars. At the far end of the cellblock, barely in sight, an imprisoned arm was wrapped around his throat. Someone; a woman, Cortney thought, held the Russian pinned to the bars of her cell door, as the sympathetic captor picked up something off the ground and disappeared to the sound of running footsteps.

The woman railed.
    "Unlock the door, you son of a bitch."
The man coughed, and stuttered.
    "Ka, ka, key is broken."
    "Unlock this door, or I'll snap your neck."
    "Key is broken," he pleaded. "Ask girl for yourself. Girl, tell her key is broken. Tell. Please tell."

Cortney pressed her visor to her own bars to watch the Russian pay, with his life, for some unknown transgression. But then her *Christian* kicked in. And she pleaded for her capture's miserable life.
    "He's telling the truth. The key is broken here in the lock."

Cortney didn't expect to hear the man's neck snap like a broken branch. And then the sound of ripping fabric proceeded some dark liquid, pooling on the ground. *Blood. Discolored by dim light. She must be stabbing him.*

*****

Nadia was in mid-sentence when a radiation suited operative burst through the door of her ready room. She pierced him with her eyes, before noticing the digital camera in his hand.
    "Back so soon? Is that it?"
    "Yes mistress, but…"
    "Is she secured?"
    "Yes, but…"
    "Then what are you babbling about, Robert?"
    "Doctor Heinrich killed Karlov."
    "And how did you two clowns allow it?"
    "He got too close to her cell door."

131

Nadia took great pleasure in knowing that the man she'd sent to lock Cortney away feared for his life. She let him squirm awhile, before bursting into laughter.

"So, Helena has joined our race. And she sees that we *do* reproduce."
Most of the room laughed with her.

"Take the girl's picture to the peace talks."
Robert gave a puzzled look. To which Nadia answered:

"Take it now, you idiot! I'll attend to Helena, myself."
Robert turned for the door.

"Wait!" Nadia stopped him. "Give me the key."

"I, I..I don't have it?"

Nadia felt a dagger pierce her sense of control. And she pulled .45 caliber Glock pistol from the holster, slung low, on her left hip.

"Where is it?" She asked and put the barrel to Robert Connelly's visor.

"It broke off in the lock. Karlov did it. I swear."
She beckoned two enforcers with her forehead.

"Search him!"

Two Valmpir patted and squeezed at Roberts radiation suit. But Nadia grew impatient.

"I mean *really* search him."
At that, the heartless goons ripped open his radiation suit. Nadia stretched out her hand for the camera. Robert gave it to her. The search turned up no key.

"Hold him here."

"Please, Nadia, please...give me another suit."
A tear slipped from his eye as they ripped off his hood. And it wasn't the first time she'd made a grown man cry.

The missile team's commanding Colonel's gloved hand was in the air.

"What?" Nadia snapped

"Please reconsider Mistress. We are not ready. If we move the launch date forward, all the missiles must be reprogrammed."

Nadia pointed her Glock and summarily executed him.

"Any more objections to a forty-eight-hour countdown?"
As she expected, no one answered.

"I understand the complexities of launching a nuclear arsenal as well as any person here. I understand the risks. I do not expect every missile will hit its intended target. We calculate seventy one percent reliability in forty-eight hours. But here is what I *do* expect. A five-megaton warhead will detonate at one thousand feet above that college hospital in forty-eight hours and fifty-two minutes. Major Tusaunt!" She shouted at the missile commander's replacement. "Have your men start the countdown. *Simultaneously*, retarget the next missile, after the decoy, for that hospital! I want those warheads exploding in America, on Sunday, while their Christian church bells ring. Am I understood?"

"At your command," Major Tusaunt said in a French accent.
He saluted and made for the rear exit.

"You two," she addressed her monster henchmen. "Come with me. And bring him along. The rest of you – to your stations!"

Robert Connelly was dragged away kicking and screaming.

*****

Cortney covered her ears at the pounding from the other end of the cell block. That cell door shook with every assault from within. A few more concussions and the top hinge flew off. Considerations raced through Cortney's mind.
Who's in there with her?
Will they help me escape, too.?
But they must be like Karen.
Maybe they'll kill me.

The door broke open at the hinge line, to the sound of tearing metal. A bloody female corpse stumbled toward Cortney's cell. Its stomach bulged like that of a pregnant woman. But clearly, this woman was well past her child bearing years. And blood dripped from the sides of her grey mouth.
Oh God, she's a vampire.

Cortney backed away as a bitter-sad, and distorted face approached the bars of her cell. The woman's eyes, and the fresh bite marks in her neck, told her story before she even spoke.
"They took everything from me. Just the other day, I was like you," she said and then looked down at her own blood-soaked blouse.

She tried straightening it as if it would help her look...human.
"I must look a mess."
Cortney was just about ready to trust, when the woman regurgitated fresh blood.
"Oh my. I *am* sorry," she said eerily.

The woman seized the bars and rattled the cell door. Cortney begged for her life.

"Please. I'm not involved in any of this. You have no reason to…"

"Hurt you? I'm not trying to hurt you. I've already drank more blood than I can stomach. Now put a shoulder to this door."

Cortney pushed, while the woman pulled. The woman put her feet against the stone wall, to better her leverage, while Cortney kicked the door. The door didn't budge. Hope escaped the younger of the two. *They'll be back down here, as soon as they hear that their man was killed by her.*

"Is that the key?"

"Huh?"

"The key is right there in the lock," the woman laughed.

"But its broken."

"My name is Helena," the woman said as she reached for the stub of the key. "Remember me."

The lock opened with a clank. Proceeded immediately, by the sound of running footsteps down stone steps.

"Run," Helena said pointing in the direction opposite the steps.

But Cortney's Christian heart delayed her.

"What about you?" She asked Helena.

Helena shook her head.

"It's too late for me. Run."

A tall woman and three men rounded the far bend. None of them wore radiation suits. Helena ran towards them, picking up the twisted cell door on the way.

"Run. Girl!"

Cortney took off, but she heard the crash of battle when the mob met Helena's battering ram. *Four vampires to one.* She wouldn't get much of a head start. She sprinted as fast as she could, for as *far* as she could, until masonry gave way to a natural cave. And feint light faded to darkness. But in that feint light, she'd passed two dark passages. She ducked back into the last one.

CHAPTER 36

Cortney tried to calm her pounding heart, lest her loud breathing give away her position. She never envisioned needing to use the Zen breath control, taught to her by Mitch.

"First bite goes to the one that finds her," a woman shouted.

"Yes, my queen," came an answer.

Nadia. Cortney was less than fifty yards away and heard Nadia's warning clearly. Her path sloped upward and became too narrow to stand. She was slowed to crawl. Then the crawl turned to a climb, as the incline increased, and the dimming light faded into darkness. Nadia's guards had reached the mouth of Cortney's tunnel.

"Check in there!" Someone shouted.

"It will be easy if she chose this path," another replied, and then laughed.

Cortney heard his laughter get louder as he entered the shaft. And she climbed up through the craggy and ever-narrowing cave. When she reached an obstruction, she understood why the man had laughed. The cave was a dead end. Cortney's heart sank as her hands surveyed the impassable boulder. But she climbed atop it and stood perfectly still.

*****

The mutant's flashlight was already dissolving the darkness, and the cave gradually turned from black to limestone green. As he climbed, the interplay of light and crystallized limestone turned into a semi-luminescent void. *She must be here, I can smell her.*

*****

Cortney saw a flash light beam pan round the boulder from her vantage point in a hollow above the cave. She wouldn't have even known it was there, had she not stood on the rock. She hoped the lip of the hollow blended, indistinguishably, into the roof of the cave. She trembled when the vampire sniffed, thinking the sound of her pounding heart would surely give her away.

She didn't move a muscle; she couldn't, until the guard's footsteps and the reflections from his jiggling flashlight faded in the distance. When it was pitch black she only relaxed, still afraid to move, fearing that the monster was trying to trick her. She heard voices at the mouth of the passage but she couldn't be sure whether or not the man-thing who followed her into the cave was one of them.

She scooted backward on her hands and seat. One, two, three times she slid backward. She had gone just a few feet, when her back pushed into a large soft surface. Reaching behind her, she determined that she'd backed into the fur of a very large animal. *A bear? Come on God.*

Cortney brushed her hand across it again, just to make sure her gloved hand wasn't playing tricks on her sense of touch. *A bear in hibernation?* This time, it moved. She shook her head in the darkness. *It can't end like this.* Agonizing seconds passed as she processed. She finally realized that the fur had not actually moved, but had given under the pressure of her touch. She almost laughed when she pushed on the fur again. *A bear's skin.* Turning around on hands and knees, she crawled past the skin, which hung over the opening to another passage. When the skin fell closed behind her, it muffled the voices of her pursuers.

Now she felt safe. Someone had been here before her, perhaps to hide also. Cortney decided she had better figure out whose dwelling she was trespassing in. It might belong to a vampire. As suddenly as the feeling of safety had come, it went.

She tried to determine the height of the roof. She was surprised to find that she was able to stand. Stretching out both arms, she found she could touch no wall. She walked from the animal-skin doorway with outstretched hands. Just as her hands touched the rear wall, her foot kicked something on the floor. Three soft musical tones chimed from the object. Cortney looked toward the opening, knowing that the animal skin would absorb the sound as it had the voices. She stooped down and carefully surveyed the object, with her hands, in the darkness. *A wooden box. A music box.*

She found the latch and slowly opened the lid. One more note played. Feeling around inside the box, she made mental pictures of its contents: paper, pencils...and a small round metal object. She picked up the small can, about the size of a spool of thread, and shook it. Something rattled inside. Twisting off the top, she poured the contents on the palm of her glove. *Wooden sticks?*

Not sticks – matches. She scraped the end on the rock floor. Nothing happened.

"Come on," she whispered, as she turned the stick over between her fingers.

She scraped the other end on the floor, and sure enough, a small flame found life. Limestone and quartz caught the match light and amplified it, like a diamond it sunlight. The chamber shimmered in a turquoise-green glow, giving it an otherworldly appearance. As the flame neared her finger, she lit a second match, and looked around for a home for the flame.

Her search lasted only a second. She was surrounded by dozens of multicolored candles, all set on ledges that had naturally formed in the walls of the cavern. She chose a purple one and gave it the light. Now she looked all around in amazement. The flickering candlelight danced against the crystalline rock and brought the interior of the cave to life.

Sparkling reflections swirled in gleaming pastels as the flickering flame struck crystals at various angles. Candles of all sizes, shapes, and colors sat in various stages of consumption. Some were made in the likenesses of animals. Some of the larger ones left intricate drip patterns that ran down to the floor, while others had never been lit at all.

The walls were also lined with little ornaments. Every nook and cranny was home to one of the little icons. Believing that one of small statues symbolized the Virgin Mary, she concluded that they must have held some religious significance. Again she felt safe...again.

The chamber was round; about eight feet in diameter. The floor sank toward center of the enclosure, and circular walls narrowed at the top and curved out of view. Another bearskin rug lay off to one edge of the circle, and on it sat a faded lavender pillow. Cortney lit two more candles, then ducked under the bearskin to make sure the light couldn't be seen from outside. She sat down on the thick bearskin pelt and cradled the pillow to her bosom.

A beautiful doll with a porcelain face sat propped at the edge of the bearskin. It was obviously very old, as it's silk and lace garments were all faded. Cortney lifted her head and scanned the dwelling, taking silent account of its contents. She spotted two pots and a tin cup on one of the larger ledges. A small metal bucket sat on the floor beneath them. A larger wooden pail with a lid on it was on the floor, further around the curving wall. She saw a pile of what appeared to be small logs. *Firewood*. Condensation, exhaled through her filter baffles told her that the radiation suit was keeping out the cold.

She saw the ash-laden depression at the base of the wall that had been used as a fire pit. Wondering how the smoke would have escaped, she looked up to see smoke-stained upper walls curve into a natural vent. A pile of books lay stacked on the uneven floor beyond the doll. Cortney scooted over next to the doll and picked up three books from the top of the stack. Mildewed covers revealed faded titles. The first was by Tolstoy. The second was Herman Melville's Moby Dick, and the third was authored by Guy de Maupassant. Resting there, in her unknown benefactor's home, she felt a deep sense of tranquility…and privilege.

"Who *are* you?" She whispered to her unseen caretaker.

Maybe there's a clue in the music box. Inside the open box, under the spilt matchsticks, Cortney found a stack of papers bound together by faded pink ribbons tied through two holes along the edge. *A book*. Cortney's jaw dropped open as she stared at the penciled cover art. It was an intricate head and shoulder sketch of a young woman. The sleeves of a beautiful lace dress hung off the delicate shoulders and a necklace of pearls adorned her thin neck. Mousy bangs covered her forehead, and the rest of her hair was pulled back and tied in a large ribbon that extended out from behind each ear. *How odd*, that the picture had no face.

"Is this you?" She asked aloud.

The second page was written in English and dated March 12th, 1921.

"What is this place?" She whispered.

She settled into the ample comfort of the thick bearskin rug and read.

CHAPTER 37

Dazzling light flicker across the pages as she read the nearly century old diary.

I burned my Russian diaries today. I believe that I will put my thoughts in English pen from now on. It is not spoken much in this part of Russia. If they ever come here I will leave in great haste and it will take days for them to find an interpreter and even then they will not know me. After all the time that has passed, I still fear they will come and drag me from my bed and kill me. I cannot imagine a place or a time when I am not hunted. In all the world, even here in this underground fortress, this remains the only place where I will ever feel safe. Not a day goes by that I do not wish I had died with the others.

A tear formed in Cortney's eye as she read on.

Cousin V came today. I only know the date when V comes. The water was not too high and I received him in the upper parlor where we exchanged gifts. He brought a likeness of Mama's favorite icon and two new candles. I gave him a pair of knitted socks. V likes the socks I make but next I will knit him a scarf. He brought dried fruit too and more bread. I read to him from Gogol before he had to leave. V promised to come again tomorrow.

A blank space on the page was followed by a second entry.

V has not returned as of yet. As always I am concerned about his safety. He has always been the reckless sort. I waited in the upper levels for five days I think, though I cannot be sure. The servants' quarters served as a suitable abode for the time. I turned on the generator and used electric lights for some of the time. Fuel is low. V will bring more. Read to Mushka when I returned. Mark Twain is her favorite for now.

"So there are two of you," Cortney whispered.

It is still very cold even though spring is near. I long to make a fire, but I am not sure it is dark and I have no desire to go all the way up to the entrance to look. Papa taught us to live by discipline. Without discipline we are but slaves to our desires. Never ever light a fire by day. Someone may see the smoke.

Cortney lost all track of time and immersed herself in the refugee's diary. It was obvious that the writer was a young female.

...V brought perfume again. He says that a young woman should have fineries, no matter her circumstance. I tell him over and over that I would be too easy to track if I were to smell of pungent scents, but I do thank him and collect the bottles. I still love Violette. I may wear it if I am ever free...

It was also very clear that 'V' was sustaining her by bringing supplies from the outside world. Some of the gifts to which the woman referred; candles, perfume bottles and the like, Cortney could saw decorating the walls of the cave. She had yet to figure out how the woman's friend, Mushka, had come to be there or why Mushka never went to the upper levels.

...I came to visit Mushka today. I combed her hair and tied it with a pretty new ribbon...

The girl was definitely Russian and was very patriotic and also politically astute.

...Oh if we could all go back to the glorious Russia of my childhood...an autocracy pure and clean. We may have avoided war...but it was only a matter of time before the people would want a voice...why is it always about power?'

She was also very religious.

...God sustains me through all of my sufferings...for some reason God has willed that I survive. I prayed beneath the icon of the Virgin Mary...Ma ma's Easter celebrations stand out as shining jewels against the background of my fading memories...'

It appeared that 'V' expected the girl to remain in the comparative luxury of the upper levels of the lair. The girl, however, preferred the Spartan accommodations of this cave. 'V' knew that she had a hiding place, but had no idea where it was.

'V was cross with me...he doesn't understand why I leave the suites or where I go...'

There were numerous references to rising water, in the lair.

...water, always water...knee high today, waste high tomorrow...always drips turn to trickles and then to floods....I would have not found this place, were it not for the incessant flooding that one day forced me up the limestone tunnel...for some reason this place never floods...

The author of the diary was very skillful at writing in generalizations, using only an initial to identify people other than 'Pa pa' or 'Ma ma' or 'Mushka'. After hours of reading, the writer's identity was still a mystery. And something about Mushka was out of place, until:

...Played with A's toys today. Mushka enjoyed the game immensely, as the toys are much closer to her size than mine. Mushka reminded me to put them back in the drawer...

Cortney stopped reading and looked around the enclosure for a drawer. It didn't click at first, and then her eyes lighted on the music box. It had three drawers under the compartment on top. She put the diary down and went over to the wooden box and slid open the top drawer. Seeing the toy soldiers in the drawer, Cortney assumed that the gigantic jewels; some loose and some on rings and bracelets, were also toys. She picked up one of the tin soldiers and held it up to study it. When she turned to walk back to the diary, the soldier that she still held at eye level, passed in front of the porcelain doll, totally blocking it from view. From Cortney's vantage point, the three-inch toy and the fourteen-inch doll were the same size when the doll came back into view.

"So you combed her hair and tied it with a pretty new ribbon," Cortney said aloud as she took notice of the faded, pink ribbon in the doll's hair.

"Hello, Mushka," Cortney said, curtsying to the doll. "I'm Cortney. Pleased to make your acquaintance."

She took a step toward the doll, but stopped abruptly.

"Oh...sorry, I forgot," she told the doll, then turned and put the toy back in the drawer.

As she closed the drawer she noticed a dull reflection in the inside of the lid of the box. She rubbed a glove against the surface and the film of the ages smudged away, revealing a mirror. She leaned the box back until she could see herself in the mirror. The dill-green hood of the Belarussian government issued radiation suit framed the visor that revealed the face of a different Cortney Landau. One she had never seen before. The eyes that stared back at her had been forged by fire. She had been through hell, and so far she had survived it. This was a face that could be trusted when the going got tough. These were the same steely eyes that she saw as a child, when her father would return home from God knows where. These were the eyes of a hero. And Cortney was no longer afraid.

She could almost hear battle trumpets as she swung her head sharply and cut her eyes at the bearskin that covered her path. She stood up from the music box and marched to the fur covered entrance. After one bracing breath she ducked under the bearskin. She crawled straight over the ledge of the antechamber and climbed down into the tunnel.

She perked her ears to listen for voices outside. She lowered herself, feet first, down the steep incline and into the widening cave. When she finally had headroom, she stood up and walked toward the dim light up ahead. Now, she could hear Russian voices… coming closer. She estimated them to be right outside the mouth of the cave. She waited and listened as the voices of two men increased in volume and then decreased. Hearing the muffled footsteps, she surmised that they were walking past the entrance. When they went far enough, she thought she might be able to slip past them. But she heard two other voices getting louder as the first voices trailed off. *They're on patrol.*

She made her way back up the tunnel and climbed up onto the ledge. Upon entering the chamber, she greeted her hostess.
"I'm back Mushka. Guess I'll be staying a while longer."

Cortney stretched to relieve the stress built up in her muscles and joints. She messaged her side and looked around at the trinkets with renewed curiosity. She picked up the small statue of *The Virgin* and looked it over carefully. On the bottom, she saw four letters scratched into the painted enamel: OTMA.
"OTMA?" Cortney questioned aloud. "Who's OTMA?"

She put the icon back on its shelf and continued looking around. Her eyes came to rest on what looked like a golden egg. And she took it from its perch. It *was* an egg, and it was covered with the same fake gems that she had seen in the drawer of the music box. But even when she held it right in front of her eyes, it still looked like it was made of real gold. *Why would someone go to the trouble of making an egg from gold and then put toy stones on it? Wait a minute.'* she thought, remembering the film on the mirror.

She rubbed the egg in the palms of her gloves. When she uncupped her hands, the diamond that crowned the golden treasure caught the light. She almost dropped it on the floor, juggling it in her hands until she finally got a good hold. Three bands of precious stones circled the egg; rubies at the top, then emeralds and sapphires at the bottom. *What the...*

"It's real!" She blurted out.

Carefully setting the egg back on the ledge, she knelt in front of the music box. Her heart pounded in anticipation as she opened the top drawer. She picked up an olive-sized clear stone and rubbed it vigorously between the palms of her gloves. A flawless, acorn-sized marquise diamond blazed to life when she opened her hands. So intoxicating was its dazzling brilliance that it made her nauseous. *Its real. It's all real.*

She put the diamond back in the drawer and went on to polish several more pieces. There was a sapphire pendant, encrusted with dozens of diamonds. She smiled when she cleaned off a pair of ruby earrings, cut in the shape of dolphins. Looking back up at the icons on the ledges, she finally noticed that some were encrusted with gems too. There was a king's ransom here.

She plopped on the bearskin and thumbed through the diary, in search of the author's identity. She read years more of entries. She learned about the playful nature of the young woman.

...I turned off the generator and left V in the dark...he says I play too much.

The woman had been alone for years, with 'V' being her only human contact. Though 'V' was the woman's cousin, she often flirted with him and secretly wished that he saw her as more than his younger relative.

... if he had not bounced me on his knee when I was a child...maybe then he would see me differently...I do so crave the attentions of a man...

But there was something else. A repeated theme.

I feel like someone is watching me
Someone is watching...
Someone is watching over me...
My watcher...
My Watcher...
The Watcher is back...

Cortney eventually got goosebumps and looked around.

"Watcher? What Watcher?"

*****

At that, the angel Pavilax smiled. He had indeed watched over the girl in the cave. Pavilax protected her in that small cavern and helped her make it into a home. He provided her with light, helped her trap food, and find potable water. For fourteen years he never left her side. He prayed when she prayed. At times, he thought that she could even sense his presence. He communicated with her, in spirit. And sometimes when she talked aloud, as she often did, she seemed to be talking to him.

"Are you only going to watch me? I know you are here. And since you have not harmed me, I deduce you must be my guardian angel. Well, sit over there. I will read to you."

*****

I have decided that my Watcher is in truth my guardian angel...

My guardian angel taught me to hunt today. He helped me trap a rabbit. But I let it go...

I must give my guardian a name. What will it be? Maybe if I listen quietly, he will tell me himself...

'V' had been a soldier at one point in his life, and that had put him in position to save her from being murdered.

V only pretended to shoot me...I could see though the crack... the other soldiers saluted him when he rode by with me hidden under the carnage in the back of the wagon.

*****

Pavilax remembered ushering the girl to the underground shelter after her family was massacred. He made it look like she'd died too, so she wouldn't be hunted. The shelter was to have been her family's refuge in times of danger, but they never made it there. Though the underground shelter was well appointed, the girl was still afraid and sought safety in the damp, dark passages deeper under the earth.

*****

Cortney put herself in the woman's shoes. How horrible it must have been to be stripped of family always afraid, cold, and alone, never even seeing the sun. Cortney read on. In 1927 'V' told the woman that she was being impersonated by imposters.

...V says that I am famous... stories written about me...rumors that I am alive...as far away as America, people pretend that they are me...

The woman had taken to sketching in nineteen twenty-three and by nineteen twenty-six she was spending many hours per day at it.

...finished another sketch of Mushka...this one is good...saved it in the drawer where I keep my best work...

Cortney found sketches in the bottom drawer of the music box. The first picture depicted a man standing against a background of pines. He was holding up a young boy in his outstretched hands. It was obvious that the boy was his pride and joy. Neither the man nor the boy had a face.

Cortney admired each sketch. None of them had faces, except for the doll, Mushka. There were several pictures of other young women, some sitting, some standing, and still others frozen in motion. Several sketches of a couple were among the art. In one picture, the couple sat with a boy straddling both their laps. It was apparent, even though they had no faces that it was the same boy and the same man that she had seen in the first picture.

And there, at the bottom of the stack, was a picture of a winged angel with powerful masculine features. At the bottom of the picture, capital letters spelled out his name. Cortney read it aloud:
"PAVILAX."

CHAPTER 38

Cortney's eyelids blinked slowly, and soon *she thought* she was asleep. When Pavilax entered her presence, she thought was a dream. The angel collected himself, in a fashion, and pressed his face into space and time to appear in the crystal lattice of the cavern wall. And his visage shimmered and danced in purple-green hues from the light of a dozen candles. Reflections of gold dithered here and there from the Easter eggs she'd polished. *What a beautiful dream.*

She wasn't surprised when every candle appeared to self-combust. The angle's face dazzled like a brilliant three-dimensional hologram, in colors so rich that it made Cortney's mind reel. The ruffles of a hundred flames took on the tonal qualities of a voice.

"We've been waiting for you."

Cortney played the spectator.

"Who are you?"

The specter answered the spectator with a question.

"Who do you suspect?" Spoke the candles.

"You mean whom."

"Very well, Cortney. Whom do you suspect that I am?"

"Are you an angel?"

"You say rightly."

"Then you must be Pavilax."

"I am. You have nothing to fear."

Cortney laughed.

"I sorta knew that. You, being the girl's protector and all. Who was she."

"Had I told anyone, the demons would have known."

"You said *we* were waiting for me. Are the more angels?"

The light grew brighter.

"Empty your heart of fear and malice. For we are in the presence of The Holy Spirit."

Cortney was unprepared for His magnificence. She'd thought it a good *idea* to believe. But she never really considered a relationship with The Almighty.

"Pavilax?" She shivered in the heat. "What do I do?"

Pavilax answered simply.

"Kneel."

She tried,

"My...my legs won't move."

"May I help you?"

"Yes. But how?"

Cortney *sensed* the angel's legs form inside her own...and bend.

"Hey wait. How did you do that?" She asked as the angel helped her bow.

"I asked. And you allowed it," Pavilax answered.

She rose on her own.

"Why are you here?" She asked Pavilax.

"Him, to explain the unexplainable. Me, to protect."

"Explain? Explain what?"

And whoosh. The Holy Spirit, using millions of crystalline facets as megapixels, took Cortney to the ancient earth. Or rather, brought the ancient earth to her. She fell from orbit, surrounded by the Glory of His Spirit, and plunged into the dark primordial ocean. Cortney held her breath until she realized she wasn't wet.

A twinkling of bioluminescent lights stretched out in every direction. Then the Spirit magnified her sight to reveal tiny organisms; microbes that sucked in water, then blinked red when they released an infinitesimal bubble.

'What's in the bubble?' She only thought.

And the candles answered.

"Bits of an ancient atmosphere."

Then came the attacks. More complex organisms attached themselves to those smaller. Every time the original organisms sucked in water the latter blinked blue. No bubbles were released by either of the microbes.

'What are they stealing?'

"You call it Oxygen."

Cortney was still underwater when the sun ignited white hot. She watched the Oxygen thieves dying. And she perceived Satan's comet, swish by from far away. A waterfall fell upwards when is passed close. The earth was dragged into a spin with the comet's coming and going.

The Spirit lifted Cortney into empty space, to watch the Genesis of creation, while at the same time outlining the trajectory of the comet.

'What am I seeing?'

"What Moses was allowed to see."

Ten thousand years past in moments. And Cortney watched as Satan's comet followed its elliptical orbit back to earth.

'Oh no.'

The comet split as it arched past Venus. Part of it burned its way through the mature atmosphere and explode over Northern Siberia.

"Nooo!" She screamed aloud. "Why me?"

Pavilax reappeared with an answer.

"You were destined to be here. You were destined to understand. Satan, himself spawned this evil. I will help you set things right."

And she fell asleep dreaming…of Satan's microbial plot.

CHAPTER 39

Stocker coughed up blood and writhed as nurse Brenda prepared the Propynyl syringe.

"His heart isn't beating, you'll have to…" Doctor Hardyway was about to remind her.

Nurse Brenda cut him off.

"I'll have to *jack it* into an artery."

"Have to what?" Nurse Carl asked.

"Like a pump. Here watch."

Nurse Brenda picked a distended artery, and placed the thick 22 gauge needle tip against Stockers skin. She pushed, but it wouldn't penetrate the boy's necrotized skin.

"Lean into it nurse," Doctor Hardyway barked.

The needle broke off. Propynyl ran down Stockers arm.

"18 Gauge needle, STAT. One hundred CC,s Propynyl. And let Carl inject him. Now listen up everybody. His lungs are dying as we speak. If we get on on heart bypass in the next five minutes, we might able to keep them alive. The atrium wall is perforated, and we don't have another heart. Let's get this one on ice while we can still repair it."

Brenda stared compassionately into the eyes of a living corpse before Carl put Stocker to sleep. Stockers humanity stared back.

"Doctor Hardyway?"

"What is it, Brenda?"

"He's already dead," she cried.

"No, he's not," the doctor snapped back.

But Brenda kept crying.

"He should be dead. Why isn't he dead?"

*****

Peter stirred from a fitful sleep. His head throbbed. His back was cold and sore. The first thing he saw when he lifted his head from the floor was jail bars. The second thing he saw was a brute of a man wearing shoes exactly like his. His own cold feet told the story.

"You're wearing my shoes?"

Though several men laughed, the question was only rhetorical. The big man stood up from a bench as Peter found his footing.

"You can have em back if you can take em off me."

Peter smiled inside.

"It won't go that easy for you."

Peter stiffened the muscles in his neck; a practice he'd perfected during countless hours of torture, to take the load off his cervical vertebrae. He walked through a barrage of punches, rolling slightly with each one, just to make his point.

"You punch like a girl," he laughed, before shattering the taller man's nose with his forehead.

The big man took another swing. Peter ducked under it, reached over it as it passed, and collected the man's arm under his own armpit. Peter dropped, and rolled backwards, tossing the man on his head. He heard the man's neck crack when his head hit the concrete.

Peter got up and straightened his wrinkled suit as the man on the floor twitched and died. Another man took off the dead man's shoes and sat them at Peter's feet. Peter looked around at the other dozen men in the cell.

"Anyone else wants to die over shoes?"

CHAPTER 40

Cortney was awaked by the rumble of her stomach. She discounted her strange dream as just that, a dream; thinking it only slightly odd that there were only two candles burning now. *'That was some dream. I should've brought that food. When was the last time I ate?'*

Something was different. She couldn't quite put her finger on it at first. Then it occurred to her. She wasn't the least bit afraid anymore. And she re-entered the world of the diary.

By nineteen twenty-eight 'V' was staying away for months on end. During one of these extended absences, the woman had to make an unwelcome decision.

...I have been without food for longer than I can bear...I cannot wait for V...God has not sustained me this long for me to starve...I must find food or I will die...
...Today I ventured outside the fortress...I can scarcely believe it for myself...Mushka thinks it glorious...the wonderful, wonderful sun warmed my bones and I found two varieties of fresh berries...

Within a few months, the woman had perfected the art of living off of wild game.

...The meat of the beaver, while difficult to chew is far preferable to that of the cave rat...I'll set another trap tomorrow...
  ...must be careful...a boat came around the bend after I speared the second fish...

She had learned to take care of herself, depending on 'V' less and less. There were less than twenty pages left in the book and Cortney found herself wondering how the story would end. The woman was spending less and less time in her little shelter. By nineteen twenty-nine, she was comfortable sleeping in the master suite of the upper level. In September of that year, she wrote:

...V is going away again...I think that this time he may not return at all...he has done more than right by me...I wish him well...God be with him on his journey to Siberia...

She read through to the last few pages of sparse entries. As she turned to the last page, what she saw snapped her back to the reality outside of the comfortable covey.

I have been at home here for twelve years but it is no longer safe. V has returned from Siberia stricken with some strange affliction marked by blackened skin. He dragged a corpse into the fortress and tore it open. I hid and watched with my own eyes as dear cousin V ate from its insides. V saw me and gave chase. I outran him, as I know these caverns in the dark. But he is not far behind. I have no doubt that he has turned into a gruesome butcher and will kill me too.

And then it hit Cortney like a punch in her gut.
    "Satan's microbes." *But it was just a dream.'*

Goosebumps rose under her radiation suit. She looked all around for a cue to reality.
    "It was a dream," she told herself aloud before reading the last entry.

I have to go now, Mushka. Sorry I do not have time to comb your hair this time. I will come back for you and our belongings soon, but for now I need both hands to climb the chimney.
    "That's it!" Cortney yelled with a jerk of her head.

She saw it clearly now and wondered why she hadn't noticed it before. The ledges on the smoke-covered wall above the fire pit were devoid of objects. She took the can of matches from the music box and looked for a candle. But the candles were all spent, save the two that were lit.

Cold chills shot down her spine as she remembered all the candles burning in her dream. It had to have been a dream. The other option was inconceivable.

She blew out what remained of one of the candles and tucked it in a pocket she found in the radiation suit. And the matches too.

Before taking the next step, Cortney looked back over her shoulder and gave a fond and farewell glance to the humble abode of the century-old woman whom she had come to know. Cortney had a strong suspicion who the woman was by now, but she still couldn't be sure. But she knew she couldn't take any of the treasure. It would be like stealing from a friend. She climbed about ten feet, and just as the covey was about to leave her view, she looked back.

"Goodbye, Mushka. Take good care,"
And she watched the doll slip out of sight.

*****

A hundred and eighty-seven miles away, in a hotel just outside Minsk, Judy Haynsworth was being rousted from her bed.

"What...who is it?" she said, breaking from her slumber. "I'm coming, hold on."
She cracked the door, to see the Council General himself standing outside her door.

"Miss Price, I am afraid you must leave now. There is a car waiting to take your party to the airport" he told her in a Russian accent.

"Leave? What do you mean leave? The talks are going well. This is only the first day. Why can't we..."

"Judy! We have to leave now!" Came the voice of the American Secretary of State's personal assistant, with his coat on over his pajamas.

"General Beauregard is at Cheyenne Mountain. We're at Defcon Two for the first time since the Cuban Missile Crisis. We're being evacuated!"

"Okay, Jim, I'll get dressed, just give me fifteen minutes."

"No, Judy. We're leaving right now. Just grab your coat and shoes."

*****

Cortney struggled upward through the darkness in the cramped chimney, until it intersected a wider passage. She fumbled with matches that slipped through her gloves. Several more failed to light. A finger to the craggy stone, slid in the century old soot.

"Too much soot. One last match. Which way now?" She asked her imaginary angel.
And she imagined him answering:

"The *wider* one."
'Duh, Cortney.'

She stopped after a time. *No more soot.*
Her hands shook as she held her breath and scraped the last match...twice.

But it didn't light.

"Dammit!"

And she imagined her angel saying.

"The other end; remember?"

The substrate no longer glowed of limestone, but with patterns of black coal, layered with various other colors of sedimentary minerals. When she held the candle level to keep the wax from running over the side, she saw that the flame was still leaning.

There must be a draft.'

But her alter ego argued:

'Maybe it's Pavilax.'

She answered her alter ego aloud.

"Shut up!"

She moved on with the flame pointing the way. She reached the first fork and paused to see if the candle pointed in any particular direction. Sure enough, it pointed to the right. She scraped along, following her flame through the maze of tunnels, until it pointed toward a shaft that seemed too steep to follow. She held the candle up in the shaft to get a better look, but the draft was so strong that it blew out the candle. She was about to curse, when she saw light in the distance.

Cortney made her way to the light. She stopped at the edge of the entrance to a ventilation duct. *'This'll be simple. I'll find a vent cover like in the movies.'*

She hadn't gone five feet before the whole thing gave way and she came crashing down with a clatter and a bang. *I gotta get outta here.* She climbed out of the twisted duct and looked around. *'Lockers?'*

Walking around the lockers and into the light, she figured that if anyone had heard the commotion, they'd already be on top of her. When she rounded the corner, she realized where she was. She had fallen into the humans' changing room. One wall was lined with lime-green radiation suits hung on a long bar. On the other side, uniform and civilian coats and other garb had been hastily thrown across a long bench in front of another row of lockers.

Cortney spotted the exit and made for it, when she looked down at her own radiation suit. The knees and elbows were worn and thread hung from the seam that had gotten caught on the cell door. But what would be most obvious to any onlooker was that the suit was no longer green. It was smudged all over with black coal from the tunnels. If she were going to survive the next few minutes, she would first have to put on a fresh radiation suit. And as she fastened hood to the clean suit, she joked.

"Ok angel," she said in half belief. "What do I do now?"

A door lock clicked. A radiation suited man with a steamed over visor ran in. A splash of fresh regurgitation in his faceplate told Cortney why. She ran passed him and into a wide corridor. She was out the door before she saw the formation of zombies marching in her direction.

'Crap!'

She remembered what Brice did to Stocker, all by himself, and froze. *'which way?'*

*****

Pavilax put his own feet inside Cortney's, and walked her....*Am I still dreaming?*...into the only other open door in the corridor. A bank of computerized work stations faced the large animated screen in front of the room. All eyes were on her. An impatient radiation suit glove pointed her to the only empty seat.

*****

Her eyes widened as she took the seat.

'I'm in the control room.'

CHAPTER 41

Kiev Ukraine
Tuesday, 21 January 2000
2:45 AM

The pilot lowered the flaps of the Airbus jetliner, signaling the final descent into the airport at Kiev. Cold night air stabbed Gary when him and Jeff stepped off the plane into the terminal jetway. Uri smiled over his newspaper as Gary and Jeff followed the other weary passengers into the terminal.

"What took you so long?" Uri asked, folding the paper.

"We got delayed at...wait, how'd you get here so...?" Jeff was asking.

"I have my sources," Uri whispered. But we have to hurry; the terrorists have deployed the mobile missiles!"

The three showed passports as they passed through customs, where Uri gave the agent a knowing nod. And they hurried off into the snowy night, to short-term parking, where Uri had a military van waiting. Uri opened the rear door and tossed Jeff the keys. Gary and Uri climbed in the back while Jeff rushed around to the driver's door. Uri opened a small door between the cargo bay and the driver's compartment.

"Stay to the left," he said as Jeff started the engine. "Take the first exit, and keep straight across the bridge."

Uri and Gary unzipped several large duffel bags and began unloading equipment. Uri sat on the fender well while he verified that three miniature global positioning satellite receivers all read the same position and velocity.

"The target coordinates have been programmed in."

He handed one to Gary and passed the other through the window to Jeff.

He reached back in the bag and pulled out three radio transceivers. He turned them on and set them all to the same channel.

"Two-hundred-mile range! They are set to channel one!" He yelled as he handed them out. "take a left after the railroad crossing."

Jeff fishtailing in the packed snow.

"Stay on this road for a hundred and sixty-one kilometers; all the way to Zhytomyr," Uri instructed.

Jeff picked up speed and said nothing. Gary sat on the other fender well and pulled on the legs of his flight suit. He stood and pulled the olive garb up over his waist, then stuck his arms through and zipped up. Uri put on his own flight suit at the same time. The two donned boots and combination utility-flack vests. They clipped radios to their vests, then Uri reached back in one of the bags and produced two Hungarian-made Glock ten-millimeter semiautomatic pistols with four extra magazines.

"Like this," he instructed, as he unzipped two pockets in the utility vest.

He put his gun in a built-in holster, and two spare magazines in holders. Gary followed suit, then looked Uri in the eye.

"Uri, I want us to be clear on this. I'm going in alone. You'll fly diversion and cover, take out twelve mobiles, just like we planned, then you'll hightail it for the boarder and punch out. Jeff will pick you up there. Right?"

But he knew that Uri was just as bad at following orders as he had been. The truck rumbled over a bump, jostling the two pilots. Jeff apologized.

"Sorry, guys."

"Listen, Gary," Uri began, regaining his balance, "I would not do anything to jeopardize Cortney's safety. I will fly diversion and cover, just like we planned."

The three went over the details, as Jeff sped through the Ukrainian night.

Nearly two hours passed. The men sat silently for the last thirty minutes.

"Twenty more clicks, people!" Jeff yelled.

Uri pulled the radio from its loop on his vest, and keyed the talk button.

"Wolf One. Are you there?" He asked in Russian.

"I am here, Hawk Two," came a voice in reply.

"Twenty kilometers away. Are you in place?"

"Yes."

Uri replaced the radio on his vest and spoke to Gary.

"Listen, my friend. The MIG-29 is far more agile than the MIG-23 we took in eighty-four, but it tends to over-respond, so keep a looser grip on the stick. It will fly itself if you let it. And another thing. You must remember to calibrate the Helmet Sighting System…"

"Uri," Gary replied, "You *do* know I was a test pilot after I retired. I flew rocket-powered bricks, for three years."
Uri was quiet for the next nineteen kilometers.

"It's not gonna be easy getting visuals on the mobile launchers." Gary said, breaking the silence.

"Don't worry," Uri assured him. "It is cold in Belarus. Some of the crews are sure to have the engines running, to keep warm, all the way up to the Arm Command. We won't even need to rely on infrared; we'll see the smoke,"

"We're almost there," Jeff reported as he turned onto the military access road, just outside Zhytomyr.

Gary stood and looked on through the portal, amazed that they were not challenged by anyone as they approached the flight line.

"Wolf One?" Uri said over his radio.
No one answered, but two headlights flashed in the distance.

"Leonid is there, Jeff," Uri said pointing.
"I see him."

Jeff slowed as he approached the building near where the headlights had flashed; at the foot the base control tower. He came to a stop next to a military rover with two occupants; a man and a woman both dressed in fatigues and heavy field jackets. The driver of the rover climbed out and approached the van. Uri opened the rear door and climbed out to meet him.

"Hello, Nephew," Uri said, in Russian, to the young man.

"Hello, Uncle. You have come a long way. It is good to see you again after all these years."

The two men hugged each other, then held shoulders at arm's length and stared at one another.

"It is good to see you too, Leonid. You look just like your father."

"You look like my father also," Leonid said, and the two of them smiled. "He asked for you…on his death bed."

"Sorry I could not be here."

"I wish we had more time to get reacquainted, but we must move quickly. You must be airborne before dawn," Leonid told him.

Gary and Jeff exchanged glances on the Van steps. Uri hadn't told them his brother's son would be an accomplice.

"And which of you is the librarian that is going to fly a MIG?" Leonid asked, in English, smiling at Jeff and Gary. Jeff answered.

"My friend here flew your uncle's MIG-23 to teach American pilots Russian dog-fighting techniques when you were probably still a kid."

Leonid nodded, and then motioned for a girl to join them. He held her hand to help her into the back of the truck.

"Who's the girl?" Gary asked Leonid, with a hint of concern.

"A distraction," he replied, with a look that headed off any further questions. "Two jets are prepared according to your specifications."

"And no one questioned your orders?" Uri asked with a furrowed brow.

"I told them they were for a weapons test exercise."

*****

Leonid nodded at the woman. She only winked at him as they exited the Van. When they'd climbed the stairs and entered the control tower, he introduced Contessa. The two male tower operators seemed puzzled.

"What is the meaning of this?" One asked in Russia.

"A gift," Leonid answered. "For not reporting my mistake last month."

When Contessa unbuttoned her blouse...they were immediately turned to sheep. Leonid left her to her work, smiling as he descended the stairs. He drove the rover to the maintenance hangar, to make final preparations for a speedy takeoff. He watched his uncle drive his van onto a side road.

He began by looking over his team's paperwork. Every item on the list had been checked off. A visual inspection of the jets verified that they had followed his orders to the letter. When the walk-around was completed he hooked a tow tractor to the front landing gear of one of the jets. He towed the plane clear of the hangar, stopping near two camouflage-colored power carts on the taxiway. Returning to the hangar, he pulled the other jet out to the power carts.

He dragged the massive black power cable from one of the carts, opened a door on the fuselage of the jet numbered 004, and plugged the large square connector into a receptacle. When he pushed the button on the side of the cart, it's diesel engine roared to life. The cockpit of 004 lit up, from the lights of dozens of illuminated indicators. Leonid climbed inside and began powering up the various onboard systems. As he worked, he contemplated his future.

He was about to follow in his uncle's footsteps. Uri had been branded the worst kind of traitor. He'd actually given the enemy a functioning piece of Russian technology. In Leonid's father's house, however, Uri was secretly revered as a hero. He had been told many stories of Uri's heroism; that his uncle had actually helped bring an end to Soviet totalitarianism. Yes, he would do this thing his uncle had asked him; for the stakes were just as high. His country once again faced nuclear annihilation, because of another country's ambitions.

Leonid powered up the Main Armament Control Panel, outside of his left knee and monitored its initialization progress on the transparent heads up display that was situated directly between the pilot and the cockpit windshield. He donned the flight helmet and turned a rotary knob, on the control panel, to the Helmet Sight Mode position. *'My uncle is my size. I can calibrate his helmet to save him time.'*

Leonid turned his head to various angles, as the weapons computer calibrated the Optical Sighting System to the position of his head. He'd have to remember to tell the American to recalibrate for his own body size. Leonid was done with the first plane in less than an hour. Then went on to power and prepare the second one; tail number 223. When he was done he left a system integrated flight helmet on the seat of each jet. Leonid left the planes powered and ready for ignition. He returned to the base of the control tower at a quarter past five, and waited outside for Contessa to come down.

At five-twenty-five, the door opened, and Contessa stepped out looking very pleased with herself. She zipped up her flight jacket, and climbed into the rover.

"Mission accomplished," she reported, with mock military bearing.

"I never doubted you," Leonid replied.

"Wolf One?" His radio whispered in the clear crisp night.

Leonid didn't answer but flashed his headlights.

"Our friends are here, Contessa. We will drop you off in town shortly," he told her as the van pulled up.

"I'll drive the rest of the way," Leonid told Jeff as he climbed the steps.

*****

Jeff got in the back with Gary, Uri, and Contessa, while Leonid drove them to the taxi ramp. The four airmen circled MIG 004, as Leonid walked Gary through the preflight inspection. Gary started up the ladder toward the cockpit. Jeff gave a slight tug on the pant leg of Gary's flight suit. Gary paused without looking down.

"You're forgetting something, old friend."

Gary heard Jeff's bass voice clearly over the diesel engine of the power cart. Gary still didn't look down, but rubbed the head of his former crew chief, just as he had done in the old days.

"Ya know, I never liked that," Jeff confessed.

"I know you didn't," Gary said, looking down into Jeff eyes now, and with the slightest of smiles, he added, "But it always brought me back safe."

Gary picked up the helmet, swung his foot into the cockpit, and climbed into the pilot's seat. He put on his helmet and yelled to Leonid as him and his uncle circled 223.

"Did you sight my helmet?"

Leonid didn't get a chance to answer. The blare of sirens filled the air. Jeff yelled up.

"They're onto us!"

"URI, WE HAVE TO GO NOW! Gary yelled at the top of his lungs.

Uri cut short his preflight and scrambled up the ladder. Jeff and Leonid snatched off the ladders just as the pilots hit the "Close Cockpit" switches.

"Uncle. Your Helmet Sighting System is already calibrated, but the American..." Leonid shouted, just before Uri's cockpit snapped shut.

Gary hit the ignition switch first. Twin turbine engines wound quickly to a high-pitched whine. As Jeff yanked the power cart cord out of the fuselage of 004, Uri hit the ignition switch of 223. Jeff and Leonid snatched the chocks from under the wheels of each jet, waved the pilots off, and jumped into the van. The two jets rolled down the taxiway as the van sped away.

Gary saw crews running toward the jets at the alert pad. One of the pilots was hopping along pulling on a boot, while the ground crews ran toward the power carts. Gary scanned the controls from left to right, translating the Russian text in his head as his eyes swept the cockpit. Another scan, from right to left, and he had it...all of it.

Uri and Gary looked toward each other as they rolled, and though they were unable to see each other's eyes through the pre-dawn darkness and the tinted visors, Gary figured they were thinking the same thing. *We may end up in a Ukrainian dogfight.'*

They swung onto the active runway, pushed their throttles full forward and hit the afterburner switches. A pair of pulsing blue flames extended three times the length of each plane, and the force of the acceleration threw them backward in their seats. Gary saw a commotion in the half-light of the control tower as they sped past.

*****

Inside the control tower, a Ukrainian colonel ranted at the two tower operators, who sat naked and ashamed.

"What in the hell has been going on here? The world is on the brink of nuclear annihilation, and you sit here naked and drunk! We have been trying to call you! The Belarussians are about to launch a strike! Are you homosexuals?"

*****

Uri and Gary were twenty feet off the ground when they ran out of runway. Uri pulled his MIG up and rolled out left, to a northwesterly heading that would take him into western Belarus. That would buy time for Gary to take out the transmitter complex. As Uri climbed, he saw Gary's MIG going straight up, spinning like a drill bit in a maneuver called an "eventail."

*****

Inside Gary's cockpit, he was being crushed by the weight of what felt like an entire defensive line piled on top of his chest. He struggled to fill his lungs with air, and felt every day of his fifty-one and a half years. He hadn't been in a fighter in six years. He had a precious few minutes to get back the stuff that once flowed in him. The target would be under him in about seventeen minutes. As he climbed, he reached a heavy hand to his countermeasures console and turned on the broadband jammer. This, to confound the radars of the control tower, and the jets that he was sure would soon be on their tails.

He barrel-rolled out of the climb at twenty thousand feet and flew upside down until he got a visual on Uri's afterburners. And he looked for those of the alert birds. The crews must've been rusty; they had not taken off yet. Maybe there would be time after all. Gary turned off the jammer so he could communicate with his team.

"Hawk Two; Hawk One."

"Hawk Two here...you big showoff," Uri responded.

"Roger that Hawk Two...Wolf One here. What's with the eventail, Hawk one?" Jeff asked.

"Just getting my wings back. You guys okay, Wolf One?" Gary asked.

"Affirmative. And FYI, ground radio chatter says the Ukrainians are responding to the situation in Belarus. They think you and Hawk Two are part of the response team."

"Hawk Two; Hawk One. See you on target in sixteen minutes," Gary radioed to Uri.

"Roger that. Hawk Two out."

The dark sky gave way to a predawn violet that swallowed the stars at night's edge and turned to magenta at the horizon. Gary pictured Cortney; taking her by the hand and pulling her to safety.

Suddenly, a thin pillar of sunburst yellow streaked skyward.

"Gary, Gary, DID YOU SEE THAT?" Uri's voice came blasting over the radio.

"I saw it, Hawk Two. ETA to target, six minutes," Gary said calmly.

The ICBM left a trail of condensation as it arched north-westward.

CHAPTER 42

As the first missile climbed, surveillance satellites from three countries squinted to track the impending doom. The U.S. went from Defense Condition Two to DEFCON One for the first time ever. And every world power followed suit. And every nuclear power automatically targeted their enemy.

General Alouicious Beauregard stood in the center of the NORAD Strategic Operations Center, under Cheyanne Mountain, in Colorado. The big, state-of-the-art Ops Screen normally displayed non-strategic trivialities. Now, it was alive with the colors of thermonuclear war. And the general bellowed.

"I want to know where that goddamned thing is headed before we set the world on fire."

"You know that'll be cutting it too close, sir. If we don't get missiles into firing sequences right now, we stand to lose half our retaliatory forces," Colonel Benton answered.

"The Russians are thinking the same thing. For Christ's sake everyone knows they only have twenty-two missiles."

Tense moments passed as the colonel coordinated verbal exchanges over a headset. The Ops screen tracked a second missile as it streaked from its launcher in an accelerating white flash, reaching seventy thousand feet in just nine seconds. The colonel listened to status over his headset.

"General, neither missile can strike U.S. soil from those trajectories."

"What about MERVs?"

"Not even with multiple reentry vehicles."

"And what about our allies?"

"Let's hope they're as cautious as you, Sir."

164

The colonel paused for a moment to listen to the communications traffic.

"We've got impact points, General."

"Well spit em out!"

"The first is headed for Venezuela, and the next one for…Northern Siberia."

"They're targeting Russia? That doesn't make any sense. There's nothing of strategic importance in anyone of those places."

The Colonel gave his own opinion.

"Russian and Venezuela are cold war allies. I'd say they're provoking a Russian retaliatory response."

"I'd say you're right. Relay that to the President.. He'll call Moscow. Maybe buy us some time."

*****

A radiation suited man, the stature of Cortney rushed into the control room, and straight for her. He yelled something in Russian. Then everyone yelled…at her. Pavilax removed his hand from inside Cortney's hand.

*****

"Sir, one of our birds just picked up beta particles in France. They're opening their silos."

"Get em on the horn. How long till the first impact?"

"Fourteen minutes, Sir. The President wants status."

"Tell him we're option one."

"You mean you don't intend to launch?"

The Colonel relayed the general's message to the President's command post, when a voice yelled across the room.

"Sir, our tactical situation display shows a bogey closing fast on the launch coordinates of the missiles!"

"What is it? And why are we just now seeing it?" The general barked.

"Didn't see it because it just took off from inside the Ukraine. It's a MIG-29, and its way over the speed limit -- Mach 2.5, Sir!"

*****

Gary removed his oxygen mask as he descended through fifteen thousand feet. He felt for the arm switch on his joystick. It had all come back in a flood. All the training, all the agony and foreboding before killing an unseen enemy by order of his superiors. But this time there was no foreboding and

165

there were no orders.

*****

"Sir, he French intend to launch against the aggressor, and silos are open all over Mainland China!" The colonel shouted the obvious.

"And there goes Russia," the general said as red arrows vectored Russian launch coordinates. "How many?"

"Twenty-seven, sir," came an answer.

But Russian arrows kept lighting.

"Now, forty-one, one twenty…"

"Never mind, Captain. Initialize launch sequences on my orders. Duane? He turned to the Colonel. "Looks like you were right. Inform the President., he's got twenty-three minutes to get everyone he cares about into a fallout shelter."

The colonel took off his headset.

"Beau, the first family has been underground since DEFCON Two. What about the rest of our families?"

"We can't put the entire U.S. population undercover, Duane, you know that." After a pause he added. "You've got thirty seconds. Call your wife. Tell her to get the kids to the Pentagon. They're safe if they make it before the outer gates come down. And, Duane?"

"Yes, sir?"

"If they launch on the Continental United States, those gates will close automatically."

"I know. What about your family, Beau?" The colonel asked as he reached for the phone.

The General scanned the humanity in the control room and said somberly:

"What kind of monster would I have to be to save my own family while I push the button on a hundred million others?"

The general looked back toward the situation board, and the colonel hung up the phone…without making his call.

*****

Gary maintained seed to pick up time closing on the first target. Denser air slowed him to Mach one-point five as he descended below five thousand feet. He'd still be going way too fast when he got there. He'd have to get rid of hundreds of knots of air speed…and right now. He was at fifteen hundred feet above the trees when he backed off the throttle and pulled the nose up into an all too high angle of attack. At the same time, he opened the airbrakes to retard his upward velocity.

The librarian got the MIG to stand up on its tail, and pancake flat across the sky. The stall warning went off almost immediately, and that's when most pilots would have dropped the nose. But Gary held it for a full seven seconds. He used throttle in combination with every control surface on the plane to balance the aerodynamic forces that held the MIG in this unnatural attitude.

No other pilot had ever been able to start this maneuver at just under the speed of sound. And even at lower speeds, no one else could hold that attitude for more than a couple of seconds without the plane tumbling, spinning, or breaking up. It was Gary's signature move.

*****

"Sir. The MIG is in a rapid deceleration," a radar operator shouted. "He's at eight hundred knots...no three hundred...now one-fifty."

"That's impossible," Colonel Benton commented "It's coming apart."

A broad grin washed over the general's face.

"I guarantee you it's possible, Duane," the general beamed. "The maneuver is called a Full Landau, and there's only one man in the world that's ever been able to hold it that long. That's Colonel Gary Landau out there; U.S. Air Force retired. Pass the word and see if there's anything we can do to give him a hand."

*****

Gary held the Landau until his gut told him he was at a hundred and thirty knots. He righted his attitude and fished the Global Positioning Receiver out of his vest. He was seven kilometers past the target, and lost more airspeed in a tight right turn. He was about to switch on his Helmet Sight Mode when he remembered that Leonid hadn't answered. He'd be off by several meters at such a close range. He switched Armament Control to "Home on Transmit", but the Heads-up Display showed transmissions emanating from all over the place. He'd have to eyeball it and get a laser lock. The sun had not yet broken over the horizon, as Gary came in from the east and squinted to find a visual clue amidst the snow covered trees. *Come on, come on...'*

And then...by that dawn's early light, he saw it — an almost imperceptible glint of metal.

"There!" He said aloud.

And he pointed the nose right at it, until he could push a HUD pointer over the target and activate a laser-aimed missile.

*****

Pavilax nodded his approval (from both near and far). It was the shiny new razor wire that Nadia had installed around the compound to keep out the local Valmpir. Pavilax *shrank* back to protect Cortney.

*****

With the target locked into the Inertial Tracking System, Gary pulled up on the nose and fired the missile as he passed. The missile shot out ahead of the plane, made a wide arching sweep, and turned back into the target. Gary couldn't see it, but he heard the explosion and his display showed an X flashing where the target had been. When he swung around he saw the antenna complex ablaze.

*****

Inside Nadia's lair there was yelling and confusion. Nadia, wearing jungle fatigues and combat boots, yelled at her operatives.

"WHY AREN'T THEY LAUNCHING?"

"We are under attack. An air-to-ground missile took out the transmitter. We cannot transmit the launch commands," a cowering man in a radiation suit answered.

"The launch sites are all manned. Contact the crews!" She screamed.

"But, madam, the transmitter . . ." someone reminded her.

"Then use your cell phones, you idiots!"

*****

Cortney's ears perked as men released her, to fish for cellphones. *Cellphones?'* And one fell at her feet. She scooped it up and eased towards the door.

"Nobody leaves!" She her Nadia yell.

Cortney took off a glove and dialed in stealth.

'Come on, Dad. Pick up.'

"Hello?"

"Uncle Jeff?" Cortney whispered.

"Cortney?"

"Where's Dad?"

"Blowin the shit outta your captors. Where are you? Did they give you a radiation suit?"

"I have on a suit. I'm here. With *her*. Everybody's yelling. Dad blew up their transmitter."

"Can you get away?"

"I don't think so."

"Listen closely, Cortney. You're in the control room. Gary's gonna punch and come for you. Can you tell us how to get there?"

"Half way down a long wide hall with doors on both sides."

"Got it. Leave the phone on. But hide it."

"One more thing, Uncle Jeff..."

Nadia's operators scurried about, making phone calls. Cortney stayed near the door, while some of them exchanged nervous glances from across the room. A man who seemed in charge yelled.

"Roll out the anti-aircraft guns. Shoot the sons of bitches down!"

*****

"General! The MIG just fired a missile into the center of the launch arsenal!" The colonel yelled into his mouthpiece.

"Well, did he hit anything? Maybe this'll buy us some time with France and China."

*****

Gary saw a column of white smoke in the distance, and remembered what Uri had said about the crews keeping the engines running to keep warm. He switched his Armament Control to Infrared, and locked the right outboard missile onto the target. Just before firing, he contacted Uri.

"Hawk Two, Hawk One. What's your twenty?"

"Hawk Two is forty clicks west of your position, Hawk One . . ."

Gary fired on the first launcher as Uri finished his transmission.

". . . I'll be there in three minutes."

*****

"He's fired another missile, General. Battle Control reports he just took out one of the mobile launchers."

As colonel Benton's words hit the air, the general's control room broke out in cheers and applause.

"There's another MIG closing in on the theater, Sir!" The colonel reported.

*****

Uri spotted the exhaust from the two westernmost mobile launchers. He turned his helmet toward each one in turn, as a pointer flashed inside the plastic of his helmet visor. He pushed a button on the throttle twice, and locked a missile onto each target. He unleashed a missile from each wing simultaneously.

*****

"General. The second MIG just took out two more mobiles," the colonel said, to more cheers.

*****

Uri's Helmet Sighting System made him far more efficient than Gary, and he was out of missiles before Gary, who had arrived on the scene first.
"Hawk one, Hawk two."
"Hawk one here."
"Tactical weapons deployed."
"Nice shootin, Hawk two. I'll take it from here."

Uri was eight for twelve, but he couldn't be a diversion for Gary without missiles, so he flew in close and peppered the complex with machinegun fire.
"Hawk two, Hawk one. Tactical weapons deployed. Get outta here, Hawk two. I got this."
"Not a chance, Hawk one. You missed the power transformer."
"Forget it, Uri. Take out the door, and get outta here."

*****

"Sir! The MIG's have taken out thirteen mobile launchers. The French and the Chinese are prepared to wait and see what happens."
"Very good, colonel. And so are we," the general answered. "Kick ass, Gary," he said under his breath.
"Sir, there is a squadron of Ukrainian MIGs, circling at the border. But..." the colonel paused, as he listened to the rest of the transmission in his earpiece. "...but they won't cross the border and attack a sovereign nation."
"We'll see about that! Patch me through to the President.!" The general ordered.

"Sir, there's more. It's the French. They can have a squadron of Mirage fighter-bombers on the scene inside of an hour, but they won't move on it without assurances that the Russians will not launch a counter strike on behalf of the Belarussians."

"An hour? Lotta good that'll do! Where's that patch?" The general barked, not taking his eyes off the Tactical Situation Display, while he shook his outstretched hand for someone to fill it with a phone.

"Stand by, Sir. He's on the hot line with the Russians."

*****

Gary took anti-aircraft hits before he saw any tracers. Nadia's anti-aircraft gunners sprayed a hail of .50 caliber rounds at the two MIG's. Fuel spurted from Gary's right wing and caught fire.

"You're on fire Hawk one. Punch out."

"Affirmed, Hawk two. Cover me."

Uri returned fire and quickly took out one of the ground gunner crews.

*****

Gary spun into a barrel roll and tried desperately to stop it. Ejecting was almost sure suicide while he was rolling. There was more than a fifty-fifty chance that he would blast himself into the ground if he tried it at this altitude.

"Gary, you will have to gain some altitude before you eject!"

"No time, old buddy. I need you to blow out that door!"

*****

Uri saw Gary's cockpit blast away, while *he* peppered the door at the south end of the complex. A second later, Gary's seat shot out of the plane while it was on its side. The evacuated aircraft crashed into the trees and exploded before Gary's chute even opened. When the chute did open, Gary was only a hundred feet above the trees. And it deployed sideways, only managing to slow him slightly before he hit the trees. *God be with you, my friend,* Uri thought, as he banked left toward the next mobile launcher.

*****

"One of the MIG's has been destroyed sir," the colonel said, dropping his head.

"Which one?"

Colonel Benton repeated the query on another voice channel.

"Gary Landau, Sir," Benton finally answered.

The general lowered his head and stiffened his jaw.

"Sir. The President," an Air Force sergeant as he handed the general a secure cordless phone.

CHAPTER 43

Angels lamented as the first missile reentered the atmosphere over the Atlantic coast of Venezuela. It screeched across the sky, and airburst at ten thousand feet. An orange-white fireball blinded every onlooker. The heat from the blast incinerated the forest below. And a blazing inferno spread like spilt molten lead for sixty miles in all directions. There would be no daylight here, come morning. At high noon the sky would still be choked black into night by the smoke.

*****

"Yes, Mister President. We monitored the detonation," the general said. There was a long silence as the President took charge of the conversation.

"Yes, Sir. That *was* our man over there, but my Colonel just informed me that the second plane has also been shot down...The scientists are correct sir. A limited nuclear exchange is survivable. It will *not* initiate a *Nuclear Winter*. But, with that much fallout in the atmosphere, there will surely be *Nuclear Autumn*."

*****

Stocker lay on his back wondering if he was nearing the end of his time on earth. He should have been angry or afraid, but all he could think of was how he had let Cortney down. If this were the end, he would either be joining her in death, or he would reach out from the grave to protect her. He swore it. Just three days ago he had a future, a beautiful friend, and a life that was all he could have hoped for. Now he was at the edge of doom. He closed his eyes, and as he drifted away, tied to *this* world by the swish of the artificial heart.

Tobias hung his head…for a moment.

"Okay, let's get to work. Scalpel, Brenda, make it a three."

Brenda slapped the scalpel crisply into his outstretched hand.

"We've been given a second chance people, let's open him back up," Tobias said as he made the first incision.

"Now raise the blinds and adjust the mirrors. I want sunlight directly on his chest."

*****

The second missile streaked down from the Siberian sky with a deafening roar, and plowed red-hot into the Tunguska forest floor at 1100 miles per hour. It burrowed 600 feet into the soft soil and shale, before striking bedrock and ricocheting back upward. It traveled a mile underground before the warhead detonated.

The detonation vaporized the forest for a mile and a half in every direction. The blast crater was a thousand feet deep at its center. A muddy orange fireball rose skyward. Five miles from ground zero, animals became weightless as the ground dropped from beneath them. When the ground rose again, it was as if it were a liquid wave radiating in all directions from the epicenter. As the wave crested, trees were uprooted and toppled.

What followed was worse. Nuclear physics and natural law united and gave birth to a secondary shockwave that cut under the topsoil at 200 miles per hour. An eerie black wall expanded outward. The jungle was being plowed up from beneath. An impenetrable spray of earth, vegetation, flesh, bone, and blood – the living surface of the planet was blasted into the atmosphere.

Seventy species of plant, animal, and insect went extinct in less than ten seconds. Over a hundred more would meet their demise from radiation poisoning in the coming months. Nadia had no way of knowing that she had just destroyed her creator – the source of her miserable existence.

Satan's microbes, and the tribe of cannibal mutants were no more.

*****

"Yes, Mister President. A third missile did plunge into the Pacific, off the Hawaiian Islands. But it failed to detonate… Yes, Sir. I understand my orders."

The general handed the phone back to the Sergeant.

"Colonel Benton." The general looked the colonel in the eye. "Upon the next enemy launch, we are to initiate counter strike sequence Orion six twenty-two. Pass the word."

"Confirming I understood you to say Orion six twenty-two, at next enemy launch," the colonel replied. "Beau . . . what about the Russians?" He asked, off the record.

"We didn't ask their permission."

CHAPTER 44

Nadia paced furiously, when three people in lime-green radiation suits entered the control room at a dead run.

'Here's my chance,' Cortney thought

"Close that door!" Nadia shouted. "Did anyone see the bodies?" She screamed at the first one through the door, as the two others coward at her feet.

"They found the second pilot's body among the wreckage. He was charred and still burning," came the answer.

'Please, God. Don't let it be my...'

"What about the other one?" She yelled, as she flailed a pistol about.

"He ejected into the ground, madam...he...he couldn't have survived it, so they did not look for him."

'YES!' Cortney cheered in her mind. *'It's him. I know it is.'*

But then she felt sorry for the man she'd hoped wasn't her father.

Nadia pointed her pistol into his ear and pulled the trigger.

"Now you," she turned to her control room commander. "Give me a damage report. Now!" She said, glaring at him.

"Thirteen mobile launchers were destroyed by the time we shot down the second plane, but there are no more enemy planes in the area."

"Can we continue the launch sequence now?" She asked, tapping the gun barrel on the left side of his chest.

"Yes, yes," the officer answered. "We have established contact with several of the remaining launchers. We will have more missiles in the air in...five...no four minutes," he said, looking towards the launch console. He held his breath while she decided his fate.

"Very well then. You will be rewarded, in the new order," she said, as the officer exhaled.

Two minutes passed, and Nadia shot a warning glance at the man who'd told her four minutes. It seemed the longest two minutes of Cortney's life. She eyed the door. *'Come on, Dad.'*

"Hurry *UP!*" Nadia hissed through clenched teeth.

"Sending out the next countdown sequence...NOW! Next launch in two minutes!" A suited man at the launch console yelled out.

Seconds ticked away as Nadia watched the countdown clock.

"Launch in ninety seconds. Subsequent missiles will follow in ten-second intervals," the man alerted the room.

The control room was silent, except for the faint tapping of a keyboard.

"Launch in sixty seconds."

*****

Nadia managed a slight smile. Washington would be hers for the taking. Her complex would be destroyed in the exchange. And then the Russian counter strike would cripple the U.S. But not before she was safely across the Belarusian border.

"Launch in thirty seconds," the man announced.

Nadia eyed Vladimir as he sat silent in the unseen exit to their escape route. And she mouthed the words:

"Time to go, my love."

The tapping at the keyboard stood out like thunder in the silent room. Nadia looked in the direction of the only person in the room who was not staring toward the countdown clock.

"Twenty seconds...nineteen...eighteen...," the announcer counted down in Russian.

*****

It's no use. I'm typing gibberish. "NO. PLEASE DON'T DO THIS!" The words were out of Cortney's mouth before she realized she'd said them.

"Fifteen...fourteen..."

Nadia leapt twenty feet across the room. Her black hair blew backwards as she sailed over two rows of computer consoles, and landed beside Cortney's chair. Nadia grabbed Cortney's right shoulder and squeezed it like a vise grip.

"The librarian's daughter. Oh, the joy," Nadia sneered, and then swung her pistol toward Cortney's head.

177

"TEN SECONDS!" The counter called out amidst the confusion.

*****

But the words were drowned out by the blasting of shots that rang out from Gary's ten-millimeter Glock, as he came charging into the room, dressed in his olive-green flight suit. Two slugs caught Nadia in the shoulder below her raised arm, causing it to fall to her side. Another bullet hit her squarely behind the right knee and blew her legs out from under her. She dropped the gun as she fell.

Gary checked the countdown clock as he ran up behind Cortney, who sat there looking up at him with her mouth agape. With six seconds left, he kicked Nadia's weapon under the console and looked at the computer screen behind his still frozen daughter.

"Good job, Cort," he said as he reached the barrel of the Glock over her shoulder, and tapped it on one of the computer keys. The countdown clock stopped at three seconds and a red backlit word flashed on the screen beside it. The others in the room were just as surprised as Cortney, who asked her father:

"What's it say, Dad?"

With a look of relief, he answered:

"It says *abort*."

"Dad, the radiation!" She yelled, noticing that Gary didn't have on a radiation suit. Just then the room exploded in movement. The first three men that ran toward Gary were human, and his heavy ten-millimeter rounds dispatched them quickly.

"GET HIM, YOU FOOLS!" Nadia shouted from the floor as she pulled herself up at the edge of the launch console with her good arm.

A dozen of her monsters turned on Gary. Cortney was on her feet.

"Careful, Dad. They're not sick like Karen was!"

Gary took two bold steps toward Nadia, and put the gun to the side of her forehead. All her followers stopped in their tracks.

"I've seen first-hand what a large caliber bullet can do to their skulls," Gary calmly said to his daughter. "Sit back down, Cort. We're not leaving until we've taken this place off-line."

As Cortney took her seat back at the keyboard, Gary spoke in Russian to Nadia.

"Move and I will evacuate your brain!"

*****

178

Cortney didn't understand the words, but she understood their power. Nadia didn't move a muscle...and neither did anyone else.

"Cortney, I've got my hands full here. What do you know about that console?" Gary asked, while staring at Nadia without so much as a blink.

"I don't know. I can navigate main pages, but I can't read the words when I get there. The angel...nevermind"

"So it was you that retargeted the second missile," Nadia interrupted, as a dark mushy substance oozed from her wounds. "How could you know..."

"You shut up!" Gary snarled and gave the pistol a push. "It's okay, Cort. You got this far, just do the best you can."

Cortney flipped frantically through the pages.
"This isn't gonna work, Dad, it's all gibberish."

*****

Gary counted the number of heads he could see in his peripheral vision, and prepared for the only outcome he could envision.

"Cortney," he began somberly, "if we don't figure something out, I'm gonna have to...wait. That's it. The pumps!"

"Pumps? What pumps, Dad?"

"You're at the Pump Control page. If I can just figure out how to turn off the pumps, this whole place will flood."

"You're just a librarian. How could you two know..."

"Peter the Great told me," was Gary's answer. "Right there, Cortney. Top of the keyboard, third key from the right says function abort. Press it." Cortney complied. Nothing happened.

"Did you think it would be that easy?" Nadia said smugly.
"Lay on the floor!" Gary yelled at her in Russian.

Nadia settled back to the floor and Gary backed away. He raised his weapon and took aim toward those standing between him and the exit, while taking an extra magazine from his vest with his free hand.

"Dad?" Cortney questioned.
"I don't have any choice, Cort."
"Wait, Dad, I heard something."
"Yeah, me too," Gary said, lowering the gun just a bit.

*****

Pavilax beamed joyous as a dozen modern, cast alloy, 500 horsepower turbine submersibles, wound to a stop. Each was eighteen feet tall, with a turbine engine that could displace 2000 gallons of water per minute. They were electrically driven with an emergency diesel backup mode. Peter the Great's drainage system had effectively lowered the water table by almost nine feet. Arranged in a cascaded configuration with triple redundancy, Nadia's pumps had given the lair an additional twenty-four feet of protection from the water table. They had operated, nearly uninterrupted, for the past nine years.

The control room, installed three years ago, was supposed to have been built above the intake opening of Peter's ancient aqueduct. Even if the pumps failed, the control room should have been flood proof. Due to a miscalculation, the steel reinforced concrete floor was poured nine inches too low. Nadia had the engineer put to a painful death, but did not want to throw off her timetable by pouring a new floor. To compensate for the error, the power outlets were installed two feet above the floor and all electrical circuitry was also to be kept two feet above the floor.

Water began seeping through the porous rock. The pump wells filled quickly and soon a small pool had started to form on the floor outside the door where Vladimir sat waiting.

*****

Gary watched water seep into the control room and expand across the floor. Soon, all eyes had turned from Gary and toward the door, where the water was streaming in at an ever increasing rate.

"Close that door, you morons!" Nadia shouted.

"Nobody moves!" Gary countered, in Russian, as water jutted across the floor.

It stopped at the walls beside the entrance ramp. It was an inch deep in seconds. Operatives (and Cortney) were pensive as water covered the soles of their radiation boots.

"Dad?"

"I see it."

Seconds dragged past as Gary evaluated the situation. He spotted a flaw. Then he whispered into one of his daughter's ear baffles.

"Up on the console, when I give the word."

"Okay," she whispered back.

No one moved. Gary wanted to keep it that way.

"Be still," he said in Russian, while waving his Glock. "Your equipment is on a raised floor... (he didn't mention the multi-socket power strips that weren't) ...the water will only rise as high as that ramp, and then spill out the door. You are safe. I don't want to hurt you."

When the water finally reached the tops of their rubber soles and began to soak through the coarse canvas and lead mesh, all the humans looked down at the same time.

"Now, Cort!" Gary shouted and followed his daughter's lead.

Four, in radiation suits, broke sloshing for the door. Before they could make it, the water reached the top of the plastic power strips and spilled into the copper contacts. Sparks and smoke spat out of every console. The control room occupants, except for Gary and Cortney, all shook in violent seizures as the current flowed through their muscles and brains. The humans fell to the floor with smoke coming out of the baffles in their hoods.

*****

The room darkened, as circuits shorted out, lit only by small fires in the consoles and behind the visor of one of the radiation suits. Carbon smoke, steam, and the smell of burnt flesh filled the air. Nadia knew the humans were all dead; their hearts stopped by the electricity. Nadia's kind were only stunned until their heads cleared of swirling stars.

"GET THE LIBRARIAN!" Nadia finally yelled out, but Gary and Cortney were already out the back door.

The pursuers assumed they had run out the front door gave chase. A hobbled, weak, and disfigured Nadia was left sitting hip-deep in water, amongst the corpses of twenty-three of her former followers.

*****

"Put your hand on my shoulder, Cort," Gary instructed as he stumbled up onto what looked like a small trestle, which clattered as they ran across, to the faint flickers of dying electrical fires. Halfway across the rickety metal bridge, Cortney lost sight of her father's outline. But she thought she heard him slip and fall. She certainly heard him grunt in pain.

"Where are you, Dad?"

A tapping on the rail signaled an intelligent presence.

"Dad?" She whispered. *He must be hurt.*
More tapping convinced her to turn back.

*****

When Gary's head cleared from the fall, he yelled:
"CORTNEY, NO! IT'S A TRICK!"

But it was too late. The emergency overhead lighting flickered on, to reveal Cortney in the clutches of a hunched over man with a decrepit face.
"I should kill her for your meddling," came the voice out of a face of stone.
The old one. "You don't need to do that, Vladimir," Gary said as he took a knee. "It's over. Just let her go."

Vladimir's face looked as if it would crack if he smiled.
"You think you know Vladimir?"
Cortney squirmed in his arm, with her neck in the crook of his elbow.
"Shoot him, Dad."
"Quiet, Cort. *If* you are *The Old One,* I know you were once a good man."
Gary waited for an answer. A tear slid down a splotchy gray cheek.
"Too long ago to remember."
Gary took aim from the kneeling position.
"Please," Gary begged.
The skin on the sides of Vladimir's mouth cracked as he smiled. Gary saw intent in those dark eyes and fired.

A chunk of flesh and bone flew from Vladimir's forehead. He stood there and died on his feet, like a grotesque statue. It took both Landaus to pry his arm from Cortney's throat.

Gary heard the muffled screech of a distant bird. He followed mosey overhead ducts with his eyes, and understood that the pumps had been used to lift ground water and channel it into a centuries-old concrete drain.
"This way, Cortney."

Gary splashed across the rest of the bridge, with his daughter in tow. By the time he reached her, the warm geothermal floodwater was halfway up his shin, and about to spill over into the drain.

Gary thought the pumps were turning back when he heard, and felt, a heavy metallic kick. Gary and Cortney watched in horror as Nadia wrestled

182

the nearest pump head in both her hands, and broke it free from the top of the pump.

Gary fired twice as Nadia tossed the heavy apparatus, as if it were a basketball.

"Duck!" He yelled to Cortney.

The pump-head arched into the concrete opening of the wide drain, and rumbled down with reverberating crashes.

Gary watched Nadia, while he counted the seconds. Nadia's parasitic blood oozed from bullet holes in her lower jaw, but Gary still saw fierce determination in her bitter eyes. After six seconds, Gary heard a thunderous collision.

*****

The outlet of the drain was hidden behind a perpetual waterfall. A heavy wrought iron gate covered the exit. Pavilax looked down from on high, and smiled when the pump head hit it like a cannon ball, and knocked it into the pond, some twenty feet below.

Pavilax saw through solid rack, as if it were glass. Gary retook aim after the pump head splashed. Nadia waded toward him through knee-deep water. The rising water spilled into the circular inlet as Nadia closed the distance between them. Gary nudged his daughter toward the aqueduct.

"Jump in, Cortney!" He shouted.

"In there?"

"Right now! Hurry!"

Cortney climbed up on the lip, as her father aimed at Nadia's forehead. The emergency lighting flicked out, leaving them in total darkness. Gary pushed his daughter into the spillway with one hand, and with the other, he emptied his weapon into the darkness.

Flashes of yellow-white light accompanied the cracks of Gary's gunshots, each one illuminating Nadia's slumping form for a split second. When his pistol was empty, Gary jumped into the aqueduct after his daughter.

He slipped effortlessly down the dark moss-lined conduit on his back, picking up speed as the rushing water pushed him along. A sharp curve sent him sliding upward and spiraling around the circumference of the tube, like an insect being washed down a drain.

A Russian fish eagle circled above the falls, waiting for the swirling water to churn up its breakfast. Warm water, pumped out of the lair, kept the pool at a relatively comfortable sixty-eight degrees. The big bird screeched a shrill retort when Cortney came blasting out through the falls. Pavilax held angelic arms just above the water, lest she break her back when she hit. If angels had lungs, Pavilax would have lent her his.

*****

"Ohhhhhhh Shhhhiit!" Cortney yelled as she went airborne.
She opened her eyes, expecting to be falling into some dark and bottomless pit. She was relieved to see that she was outside the lair. She was still falling though, and falling backward. Hearing the waterfall crashing into the water below, she hoped it was deep enough to break her fall. She hit the water on her back, hoping not to feel too much pain.

It took her a moment to realize that she was under water, and that the spray she felt on her face was water rushing in through the baffles in her hood. The radiation suit was already heavy from the lead lining, but now it was becoming water logged. And though Cortney was a strong swimmer, she could not keep herself from sinking to the bottom of the pool. She managed one more small breath, before the remaining air was displaced from inside her hood.

*****

Gary blew out of the falls a few seconds after he heard Cortney's splash. He righted himself on the way down, and hit the water feet first. Catching water under his outstretched arms, he pushed himself back up to the surface.

"Cortneyaaa!" He wailed, and paddled in a circle to get a better look.
Surmising what had happened, he took a gulp of air, flipped over, and kicked for the bottom. His heart pounded as he struggled to discern the various shades of green at the bottom of the pond. Cortney's strawberry-blonde hair wavering in the water caught Gary's attention.

Her head gear was off, but the suit's zipper was stuck and now she struggled to free it. She was out of air and starting to panic, when her father tapped her on the shoulder and smiled. Cortney pointed at her neck and shook her head from side to side, signifying that she couldn't hold her breath any longer.

*****

I'm drowning. Why is he smiling?

Gary grabbed her collar and opened a flap under his left armpit with his free hand. When he pulled on a cord a bright yellow airbag inflated under each arm. They were at the surface in seconds, where Cortney gulped air and clung to her father's neck.

At the edge of the pond, Gary and Cortney wiped water from each other's hair.

"I knew you'd come for me, Dad. I never gave up hope," Cortney panted through chattering teeth.

"It's okay now, honey. It's all over,"

"No, Dad, she's still in there!" Cortney yelled and pushed away.

Gary caught her by the shoulders.

"She's dead Cortney. I'm getting you out of here. Understood?"

"But, Dad, what about Stocker?"

Gary looked at the ground.

"I wish I'd been there for him. I won't lose you too. That pond is radioactive. Your suit's contaminated now, Cort. I'm gonna give you my flight suit. It's water tight," he said, pulling what looked like a walky-talky from his pocket.

"But, Dad, you'll freeze."

*****

Gary didn't answer. He was about to key the talk switch, when they heard a loud splash in the pond behind him. Lowering the radio, he whipped around to look.

"What was that?"

"I don't know, I couldn't see past you."

They both stared at the pool for a long time.

"Maybe it was a boulder or something," Cortney suggested.

"There weren't any boulders in that channel. Come on, we'd better get moving," he said, taking Cortney by the arm.

They'd almost made it to a stand of pines, when a voice called out in English from behind.

"Libraaariaaan," came a voice, feigning coyness.

Nadia's mouth was just clear of the waterline.

"We have unfinished business." she cooed, rising with each additional step.

Gary pulled Cortney along, parallel to the water's edge, while he gave her final instructions. Nadia turned to shorten the distance between them; just like Gary knew she would. It would keep her in the water longer, giving him and Cortney more time.

"Cort," he began, just above a whisper. "Your suit will get lighter as the water drains out. You head north," he said, pointing straight ahead. "As soon as you're out of sight, turn east, directly into the sun. Don't use the radio until you're sure no one else can hear. Then call Jeff," he said, showing her the transmit switch with his thumb. "Get out of the suit when he answers. Wearing this one's worse than not having one at all."

"Time for a reckoning, Mister Landau," Nadia sneered, as Cortney ran for the tree line.

Nadia was almost out of the water now, and it was already apparent that she wasn't going to be able to put much weight on her right leg.

"Keep going, Cort," Gary yelled, and then turned to face Nadia.
"No, Dad, come on. We can both make it!" Cortney pleaded, looking over her shoulder as she ran.

When Nadia finally got out of the water, Gary's hopes were dashed. Even with a bum leg, Nadia hopped in six-foot bounds, dragging her shot-out leg behind her.
"RUN, CORTNEY!" Gary yelled as he stepped toward Nadia.
But all of a sudden Nadia stopped. So did Gary. So did Cortney.

All around them, Nadia's Valley People were walking out from the trees. At first there were only six or seven of them; some naked, some dressed in burlap and animal pelts. One of them carried the hood of a radiation suit, upside down, like a grocery sack. Blood dripped from the ear baffles. It had something inside…something about the size of a human head.

Nadia turned and slowly backed away from them. Soon there were a dozen, and before long, there were over twenty of them. Wild-eyed and salivating, they herded Gary, Cortney, *and* Nadia toward the center of a large semi-circle. A young female with coils of golden locks stepped forward from their ranks. Eyes ablaze and staring straight on at Nadia, she held up a hand to stop those behind her.
"Oh, look at the Grand Madam *now*," the girl began in clear and proper Russian. "Where is your army?" She asked rhetorically, spreading her arms toward each horizon. "And where is your humanity? Where is that thin veil

of a notion that you once used to separate yourself from the rest of us? You thought yourself superior to *everyone* else. We know how you taunt and torture your victims, like a child teasing an insect before destroying it. You persecute us, forcing us to live as animals and even disdain your own followers."

Cortney tugged Gary's sleeve.
"What's she saying, Dad."
"That Nadia's a monster. Shhh."

The creature walked continually forward while she spoke. For every step she took, Nadia took a half step backward and closer to Gary and Cortney.
"And do you notice," the golden-haired girl continued, "that I have had the decency not to base my disgust for you upon the mere fact that your face has bullet holes in it? Should I consider you lesser now that angry men have ruined your makeup? It is unfortunate that we cannot derive sustenance from *your* blood. But we will destroy you anyway."

Now the others in her clan pressed forward. Nadia backed away steadily and silently.
"What's wrong, bitch?" Cortney snapped at Nadia when she was close enough. "Doesn't *everybody* answer to you? Why not just command them to go away?"

Three shades of green uniforms backed into the water; Gary in his olive flight suit, Cortney in a lime radiation suit, and Nadia in camouflage fatigues.

And Nadia wailed.
"I hate you! All of you! You are all inferior! Even now you should be bowing down to serve me! My guards will..." She was cut off by a thunderous commotion.

*****

Jeff spotted the bright yellow air bags as soon as the rescue chopper cleared the hilltop.
"TAKE US DOWN!" He yelled to Leonid, who was at the controls.
"I SEE THEM!" Leonid replied.

All eyes around the pond looked toward the beating sound of the helicopter blades. Gary pulled Cortney close to him. Jeff took to the open doorway and let loose with an AK-47. He laid strafing fire at the feet of the Valley

People, backing them away from Gary and Cortney, who moved to put distance between themselves and Nadia.

*****

Without a word, Gary unzipped a flap at the back of his neck, exposing a metal tether. Nadia realized what was about to happen and tried to move toward him, intent upon saving herself as they were rescued. Gary wagged a finger at her, and shook his head.

"This time you pay!".

Jeff blasted a volley into the water between Gary and Nadia, before activating the rescue winch. When it came within reach, Gary grabbed the hook and attached it to his tether.

"Hold on tight, Cort," he said, tightening his arms around her.

As Jeff hoisted them to safety, Gary's eyes never left Nadia.

"Welcome home," Jeff said as he pulled them aboard.

Leonid tilted the rotor and began climbing out.

"NO, WAIT!" Cortney shouted, as she leaned to look out the door.

"THAT HER?" Jeff said pointing down at Nadia, as the Valley People closed in on her.

Gary just nodded.

The helicopter hovered while the outcasts descended on Nadia like a pack of ravenous wolves and ripped her limb from limb. As they tossed her body parts back and forth among themselves in celebration, Leonid climbed out to the south at full speed.

"WHERE'S URI?" Gary shouted.

Jeff leaned in close to Gary so he wouldn't have to shout.

"Uri didn't make it."

Sometime later, a squadron of Ukrainian fighters screamed overhead on a northerly bearing. Jeff said they were under orders to level the complex. By noon, he said, Russian ground troops would be on the scene to mop up the mess.

Gary and Cortney looked on numbly, as Jeff felt around in the field pack between his legs. Cortney was bundled under a pile of blankets. Her tainted radiation suit had been thrown over the side. Finally, Jeff pulled out two protein bars and handed them to Gary and Cortney, saying:

"You guys look hungry. Want some breakfast?"

Father and daughter looked at each other and smiled.

"Cortney?"

"Yeah, Dad?"

"Did I here her say you retargeted a missile?"

"Yeah, Dad."

"How is that possible?"

*****

Cortney giggled inside. How would she explain a miracle to her father, who she'd tried for years to convince that God existed. But maybe, just maybe, he was ready to believe.

"Dad," she began.

"Go ahead. I'm listening."

"Have you ever believed there were angels?"

EPILOG

Two Months Later

Gary sat at a classified terminal in the closed area, answering what he hoped was the last of a series of congressional inquiries, when Jeff strolled in.

"Hey, guess what I just heard?"

"What's that, Jeff?" Gary asked without looking up.

"Uri was just posthumously awarded the Ukrainian Medal of Honor."

Gary finished typing his sentence and then turned around in the chair to face Jeff.

"Yeah, I was just reading about it before I came in here. They wiped his record clean. He's a national hero. I hear Leonid got a medal too."

"And he's gonna get a promotion; he just doesn't know it yet," Jeff said, and they both laughed.

"Whatcha doin?" Jeff asked, nodding at Gary's work.

"Just finishing up this statement to Congress."

"Funny how we were never even mentioned in the official report," Jeff said sarcastically.

"We were never there, Jeff. Neither was Cortney," Gary responded as he typed.

"Hard to get over the fact that Judy got credit for tipping off the Ukrainians," Jeff said shaking his head.

"At least it got her out of our hair. She's the President's problem now," Gary said as he hit 'send'. "Hey, guess what that future son-in-law of mine did with the rest of the money he hacked out of the Romanov accounts?"

"You mean after he paid the Ukrainians for their downed jets, filled government coffers in both Belarus and the Ukraine, opened up a fund for a new Library of Congress building...and bought your wife a new car?" Jeff chuckled.

"The car came out of his finder's fee," Gary laughed. "Anyway, he used the last three-hundred million to open a medical foundation to research and treat patients suffering from Stocker Blake's Disease. They..."

"Hold on, Gary. You mean they officially named the condition after Stocker?"

"Yeah, Dr. Hardyway saw to that. They've already broken ground for the first hospital," Gary said as he logged off. "I'm done here."

"Come on," Jeff motioned. "I'll walk you back to your new office."

They strolled back to the open side of the building, talking as they went.

"I hear the last of the Venezuelan fires finally burned themselves out," Gary informed Jeff. "The library's chief climatologist says next winter will be colder than normal."

"Figures," Jeff replied as they arrived at Gary's office door. "So when's the wedding?"

A workman had just finished installing a pane of glass in the door, and the two waited as he sprayed on window cleaner and wiped it off with a paper towel.

"They wanna get married this summer. Alicia, of course, is having a problem with every detail."

They laughed, and Gary thanked the workman as he wheeled away his tool cart, revealing the new inscription on Judy Haynsworth's former office door: Gary Landau Director of Russian Studies.

*****

On the other side of the country, Cortney sat on the edge of Stocker's hospital bed and ran her finger along the wide scar on Stocker's bare chest.

"It's been two months, Stocker. You're gonna have to talk about it eventually."

Stocker forced a smile.

"*You* haven't said much about what happened to *you* over there either."

"You know my father will get in trouble if I tell anybody I was there," she answered. "But maybe I'll tell you. Someday. I guess. I'm still trying to process it all. I can't tell...I mean I don't know the difference between what really happened and what I imagined. I tried to explain it to my father. But I couldn't find the right words."

Stocker sat up straight. And Cortney moved to the arm chair beside the bed.

"I know just how you feel, Cortney. Something happened to me while I was in surgery. I tried explaining it to Doctor Hardyway. He didn't get it either."

Cortney reached over and took Stocker's hand.

"I might."

"Nah. The doctor said it was just the anesthesia. I was under for sixteen hours while they fixed my heart and put it back in.".

Cortney winched

"Come on. Try me."

Stocker pursed his lips and went backward in his mind.

"It was probably just a dream."

Cortney leaned over and stared in his eyes, as if she knew what he was about to say.

"Stocker. You have my undivided attention."

"Cortney?"

"I'm listening."

"Do you believe in angels?"

.

*****

Later that night in Cortney's political science class, the professor was lecturing as the class followed along in the textbook.

"The Austrian Emperor was eighty-four years old," he was saying as Cortney walked in. "How nice of you to join us, Miss Landau. Please take a seat and turn to page 216."

Cortney raised her eyebrows apologetically, and crept to her seat as the professor continued.

"As I was saying, Franz Joseph was eighty-four in nineteen-fourteen. His only son had committed suicide. His brother *and* his wife had been murdered, leaving his nephew, Franz Ferdinand, as his only heir. That year, Ferdinand was assassinated by a Slav nationalist, and it was this act that drove Austria to declare war on the Slavs, setting the stage for the start of World War One..."

Cortney listened as intently as she could while the professor droned on. She was pleasantly distracted by thoughts of her wedding.

". . . Austria was allied with Germany. The German Kaiser, William the

Second, pictured on page 217, vowed to protect Austria if Russia came to the defense of the Slavs . . ."

God I hate this class, Cortney thought, as she turned to page 217.

". . . Tsar Nicholas the Second had no choice. He could not allow the southern end of the Russian Empire to be attacked. He prepared for war, even though the Kaiser was his own cousin," the professor was saying. "That's Nicholas, shown with his family, on the next page..."

A broad grin washed over Cortney's face as she looked at the adjacent page. The professor's words faded in and out as she concentrated on the picture.

"...his wife, Alexandra, his son, Alexis, and daughters, Olga, Tatiana, Marie, and Anastasia. The girls sometimes referred to themselves collectively, as OTMA..."

A single tear slid down Cortney's cheek. *So it's you old friend*, she thought as she stared at the youngest of the girls. Thank you for your hospitality...thank you for saving my life too, she thought as she wiped away the tear. Oh...and Mushka sends her regards.

The End

OTHER BOOKS BY MICHAEL KENT

The Haunting of Molly Pickett
Three Days after the Cross
Growing through the Cracks of Adversity
The Family Business
Deranged

Available on Amazon   & Kindle
Audiobooks available at TalesFromTheMikeSide.com

www.ingramcontent.com/pod-product-compliance
Lightning Source LLC
Chambersburg PA
CBHW060105260626
47160CB00005B/1808